
INOCULATED BY FIRE!

Kashmir: A Company Commander
Comes of Age

HARMINDER SINGH MULTANI

Largely based on true experiences, with a few suitable
modifications to gel into the overall story being told.

Title: *Inoculated by Fire!*

Author: Harminder Singh Multani

Email: harmindersingh23@gmail.com

Copyright ©Harminder Singh Multani 2020
Publication Date: September, 2020

ISBN 978-93-5416-647-1
e-Book ISBN 978-93-5419-152-7

Publisher: Self published

In the loving memory of my father
S. Gurmit Singh Multani
<u>1947-2020</u>,

Who passed into the afterlife this year.
He never failed to motivate and inspire me to achieve greater
heights while being grounded to the core.

Dedicated to my mother,

Kuldip Kaur Multani

and my family,
*especially my wife, **Suruchi Kasliwal Multani***
who have been a constant support through my journey of life.

My Gratitude

*to my brother, **S. Baljinder Singh Multani** and my nephew,*
***Divjot** who read the first manuscript and provided valuable*
inputs including encouraging me to take the book to print.

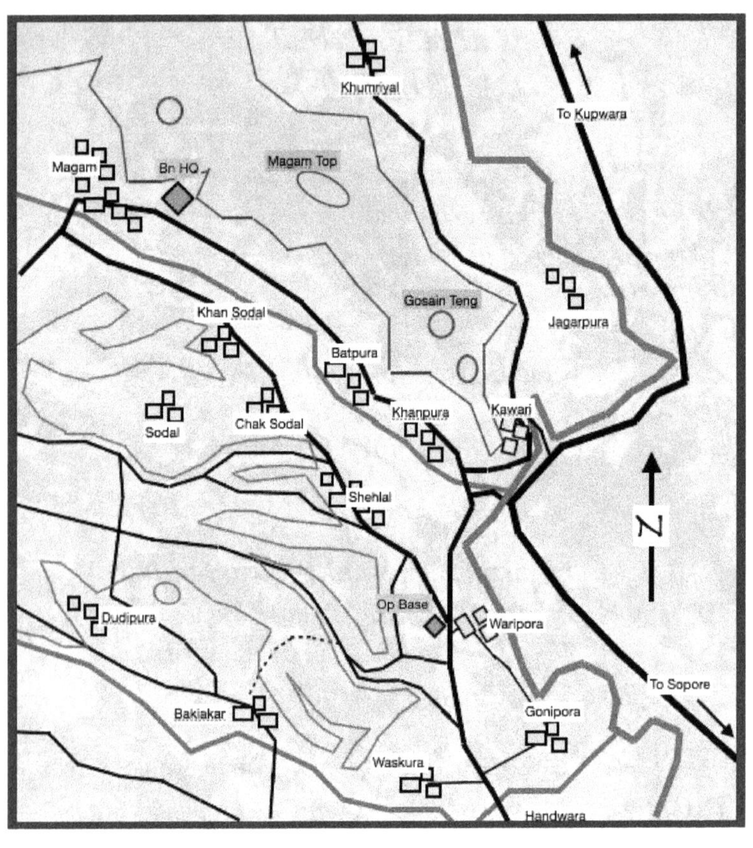

Khumriyal
To Kupwara
Magam
Bn HQ
Magam Top
Gosain Teng
Jagarpura
Khan Sodal
Batpura
Sodal
Chak Sodal
Khanpura
Kawari
Shehlal
Dudipura
Op Base
Waripora
To Sopore
Bakiakar
Gonipora
Waskura
Handwara
N

Table of Contents

1

The Early Years

"Every soldier's ultimate dream is to be tested in battle" or at least it should be. And even before that I wanted to be a soldier first. Having donned the olive greens I was no different.

I watched war movies as a kid and very soon started imagining myself in such a role - fighting the enemy for my motherland. The patriotic songs as if written specifically to motivate me.

Growing up as an Army kid, I found myself in the midst of this heady mix. As if the whole world is conspiring to send me in one particular direction. After all, developing a nationalistic character needs the kind of reinforcement where one believes that everyone else too believes in it.

Being an Army kid, finding motivation and remaining motivated to join the forces is easy especially if your dad is the motivated kinds. To be surrounded by Army men - immaculately dressed and upright I grew up in a world where young impressionable minds can think of doing little else than join the forces. After all, we are all in awe of our parents when young.

As a kid, I was risk taking and eager to do the extraordinary. I wanted to be different and one fine evening at a young age of 10 years, when I happened to see a promotional video of one of the Sainik schools, I instantly wanted to join the school. Seeing young kids do things that an otherwise normal school that I went to then did not offer, had me yearning to join. A couple of consultations and advices later, I had firmly set my eyes on getting into the top rated military college in the country which also brought me to face the first national level entrance exam of my life. That the Gods wanted me to do so was confirmed as I topped the list of those aspiring to join.

Five years of intensive training prepared me to excel at just about anything and a military career in particular. The variety of challenges at school kept me motivated and looking forward to even bigger challenges.

Finishing school in early 90s at a time when the Indian economy had just opened up with promises of lucrative and high growth careers on the civvy street, did cause certain strain on my choice of career path to which I was firmly committed otherwise. The resolve to make it to the National Defence Academy (NDA) which was considered the best way to join the forces then, came under duress. Family pressures added to the dilemma. I was under severe mental strife when I decided to depend on my destiny. Preparing very little and going through the paces of the selection procedure, I hoped that my selection would be

God's way of pointing me in the right direction. Sometimes, leaving it all on the Gods, works.

When the UPSC[1] results came, I had made it amongst the toppers of the batch which dispelled all doubts whatsoever, for destiny awaited me. Upbringing in a military school had laid the right foundation for me to absorb the training at NDA. The next three years were well spent in developing skills required for what was to come, besides making some great friends for life. The relationships and skills developed in school helped me dodge the unnecessary by-products that intense military training brings along - the kind that can become a drag on an otherwise quality oriented training. Having successfully completed the training at NDA, I was now headed to the Indian Military Academy (IMA) at Dehradun - the finishing academy for those aspiring to serve the country as Army officers.

The training at the academy was completely focused on what was to come in the immediate future. With counter-terrorism operations taking up most of the Indian Army's time in Kashmir and the eastern theatre, the training at the IMA was oriented towards preparing young wannabe officers to be successful in such an environment - after all nearly half the class was to eventually find Itself in such internal peace keeping tasks. The other half too was expected to eventually find its way into such an environment sooner than later.

---

[1] Union Public Service Commission

That the motivation levels were sky rocketing was clearly visible from the fact that almost everyone was yearning to be given a chance to enter into a combat zone and prove one's blood. Four years of training can do that. The situation in Kashmir was considerably raw and had worsened only recently then, so it was only expected to hog maximum limelight. Most young instructors at the academy were fresh out of the valley and in a state to provide first hand accounts of what to expect up there.

Hence, moving into the valley in a Counter Terrorism role became important for everyone - something no one could escape. But at the age and time in a young soldier's life, it became an aspiration. When the graduation came and everyone received their posting orders, I was amongst the half that was not immediately going into a counter-terrorism role. Instead I was going to serve in a tank regiment in the plains of Punjab - most of that time was spent in the deserts of Rajasthan though.

Having done well in my career thus far and the courses in between, I was eventually posted to the IMA as an instructor - once again back amidst the preparations for counter-terrorism operations. Every now and then an innocent question from the students - "Have you served up there, sir?" haunted me, for of course, I hadn't. A fire that had been smouldering all those years after the academy days as a cadet was re-ignited. I wanted to go to the Kashmir valley. On completion of the instructor tenure, I was once again hoping to be posted into the valley, but it was not to be, for I was nominated to the Tank Technology

Course at Pune. This in itself was a complete antithesis to what I wanted.

Once over at Pune with my peer group, I was re-united with some of my old friends. A few amongst us were returning from the Kashmir Valley. Occasionally, time was spent listening to their stories, about their experiences in the valley. I wondered how I would have reacted in those situations. As I spent a year learning the nitti-gritties of tank designing, I had completely forgotten about my nascent desire to go and experience what was up there. Pune as a city can do that to you. But then, the course was near completion, and the posting orders came pouring in for the course.

I was finally going to the Valley. A long felt secret desire was going to be fulfilled soon. I had spent two years of my childhood there while still in school and in better times as an Army kid, I wanted to see how different things could be.

2

Moving into the Valley

oving into the valley, all the stories I had heard kept playing on my mind. Besides, occasionally remembering the 'be safe' advice from the family members or was it their concern speaking. Luckily for me, I was inducting by road. That allowed me the luxury of slowly acclimatising both to the change in the air and the environment.

The older experienced hands found this an opportune moment to impress the greenhorns such as me with their knowledge and ability to handle what's up there. Perhaps the best part is where I was systematically tutored on best techniques to extract information from the suspects. Unfortunately, for the purpose, every single person of the local population is an information source and every method is fair game including third degree.

This is where I learnt about the various interrogation and torture techniques that do not otherwise exist in any manual. I wondered if any manual existed at all. No one though shared how successful they had been using those techniques. That, I believe, was left for me to experience. It was assumed that if they are propagating the technique, it had been successful.

Jammu transit camp is the first one of the transit camps enroute. Not frequented by many now. Over the years, it had lost its importance as air connectivity had become the main stay for army transiteers into the valley, leading to the growth in Delhi and Chandigarh transit camps.

"If you get in, in time, you will be quickly moved to the next transit camp in Udhampur.", I was told by my friends.

Udhampur is comparatively much cooler than Jammu and allowed me to have an easier morning the following day. I could wake up easy in the morning. Incidentally, this is where the education started too. I met all kinds of people with all kinds of opinions. The more philosophical ones seemed to have a humanitarian solution to the problem up there. The authoritarian ones seemed to have solutions that could rid the Kashmir valley of its problems much sooner, even overnight.

It was easy to get mesmerised by the tales of valour, bloodshed, tricky operations, blood and guts. But very soon, I realised that I was being fed on mostly hearsay. Stories passed down from one generation of officers in the valley to the next. After all, not everyone can be in a real life spectacular story always. I quickly learnt to discount or take things with a pinch of salt. However, one knows when one meets someone who has been in a real operation and in the thick of it.

One such real hero had been in a cordon and search operation[2] and ended up in a hand to hand battle with a terrorist in the middle of a search operation on a street in the village. A rare case where the weapon just didn't fire and the terrorist appeared at five metres from him. The battle that ensued was more of a wrestling match for survival and not to let the terrorist fire his AK-47. It took him three months post a few surgeries in the military hospitals to recover from the wounds physically. But, clearly, he was much too emotionally scarred to recover completely from the trauma of it all. The valour of course, didn't go unnoticed. He was soon to be decorated for it.

Talking of decorations, I got to hear numerous stories of people who came to the valley solely for the purpose and thus, ended up becoming more than a bad example. Stories of people who out of desperation for a medal, undertook operations that were far too risky and thus ended up paying for it with their lives. Such stories were often followed with notes of caution.

There was another variety of stories that I got to hear. Stories of reformists - people who undertook missions to solve the entire Kashmir problem by themselves, where people tried talking to terrorists to convince them to give

---

[2] An operation that involves surrounding a village housing suspected elements, followed by a thorough house to house search to flush them out at significant risk.

up their wrong ways. Unfortunately, nothing much had changed on that score too.

However, generally there was not one single advice on following a purely military way of doing things- following the training, SOPs, manuals, et al that I was taught in various training academies and otherwise. Somewhere, there appeared to be an inclination to do the spectacular - something different, something that hadn't been told to them earlier. Of course, one wanted to be a story too. It was way more romantic that way. And following the usual standard procedures and drills did not make great stories. I do think though, that those were enough to make me successful as a field commander and more importantly to keep me alive, so that I could continue to hear stories of others.

One thing was clear though. By the time I got to my area of operations, I was far too enlightened and focused on what to expect or at least I thought so. Getting to the ground, however, was a little slow and not half as eventful as it sounded. At this moment, I was also tentative, having heard all those stories, that I started to imagine a situation everywhere and in everything.

This state of mind led to a very challenging initial few months in the Kashmir valley. A period that was focused on proving that you can get the kills. Hence, almost all the time was spent pursuing just that. For a company commander (CoCo) in anti-terrorism operations, this could be an extremely risky and dangerous time. This was the time when I was so focused on what's outside the operational base (op base), that I could very quickly and conveniently forget everything that needed handling inside. The morale of the men I commanded being the one most important part. I was trained for that at least theoretically. I soon realised that maintaining high morale is easier said than done. For it involved a very large set of activities to be done right - the right living conditions, the right quality of food, adequate training, adequate rest and recoup to include leave, correct and complete personal documentation, safety and security. The list was endless.

3

Settling down in Command

T aking over command at the fag end of the calendar year in the winter of 2004 posed peculiar problems. A large number of the men had not availed leave and almost everyone who had not, sensing that time may lapse as also the leave quota for the year, was queuing up for grant of leave. To top it all, in a set up such as the Rashtriya Rifles, I did not have previous exposure to the men I was set to command. Hence, the challenge multiplied as I just didn't know whose was a genuine case and whose wasn't. With a large number of people already on leave and a set of essential duties to be performed everyday, it was a traumatic experience handling the cases. Saying 'no' to people who had some close reasons to go home was extremely stressing.

The previous Company Commander had been so focused on operations that he had completely missed out on the administrative issues of the company. However, it was best not to judge him because he alone knew his circumstances best. He was a generous old timer who enjoyed his two drinks in the evenings. His generosity, however, left the company deficient of its rations. Magnanimity comes at a price.

I somehow spent those two months saying no to excessive leave seekers, seeing my area of responsibility and mostly fighting the weather that felt unusually cold. Thankfully, this was the time, real military operations were few allowing me some breathing space to come to terms with the changed environment. The cold weather and snowed out mornings lulled me into complacency and a very relaxed command. It was an ideal setting for something to go wrong and it did.

It was a fine cold morning with gentle snow falling. The weather was all packed with absolutely no sign of sunshine in the immediate future. I had just settled down hoping for a relaxed 'nothing to do morning' after a sumptuous breakfast. After all, I could not have hoped to inconvenience the local population given the weather. And then, two shots were heard clearly, fired in quick succession. Snowfall unlike rain is extremely silent. The firing of the two rounds was deafening and it came from really close quarters. I completely froze in the midst of wearing my boots, straining hard to listen to figure out what might just have happened.

A number of thoughts quickly raced through my mind.

"Was it the dreaded 'fidayeen'[3]?"

"From which direction?"

"In broad daylight?"

"Was it a standoff attack by the militants?"

"Or worse still, had someone run amok ? After all, there had been far too many 'noes' to leave requests of late."

To what appeared like an eternity, in all of ten seconds or less, I could now hear a commotion. This got me into action to get to the point of origin. Thankfully, it wasn't any of the above. One of the boys had fired from a Light Machine Gun with the barrel pointing towards the sky accidentally. The bullets had clearly pierced through his palm as he was holding the barrel with his left hand over the top. The shots had also made a clean exit through the roof on top. Thankfully! No one's life was in danger. But the boy was hurt and needed medical attention. Everyone was looking at me. My integrity was immediately put to test. The perils of a court of enquiry on account of accidental discharge of weapon loomed large. One way out was to get the boy local medical treatment to avoid declaring the incident and thus escape any enquiry. But at the same time, the boy's hand was in question.

"What if the local medication went wrong?"

I eventually chose to report the matter through the proper channel. The boy's well being was more important-

---

[3] A term used to denote a suicide mission undertaken by the militants in the valley.

definitely over my own - at least that is what the IMA credo said.

The entire hierarchy in the chain of command learnt about the incident. The commanding officer came calling very soon. The boy after some initial first aid was quickly moved for further treatment. He, however, kept saying that he was alright and remained cheerful inspite of the injury - such was the courage and spirit of the young Sikh soldier. But his present tenure in the field was over.

The shots did shake me out of an operations focused one track mind. The incident was to leave me awake for many a days with one scenario haunting me.

"What if the barrel, when the gun accidentally went off, was pointing at someone and a precious life was lost?"

And on top of it all, the scare of the court of enquiry loomed. I was now also thinking of all those questions which I would be asked and had no real answers for, for there truly were no procedures implemented by me. Procedures such as when and where must a soldier be allowed to clean one's weapon? The irony of a court of enquiry in the Army is that it goes beyond just the incident and finds answers to questions that ascertain whether the right drills and procedures were in place to avert accidents. I was already constrained to think of what should be the right procedure.

The preparation for the impending court of inquiry made me realise all that I should have been doing in the first place - procedures I had taken for granted. The realisation that an extremely operation focused mindset alone will not do, came rather quickly. Necessity is the mother of invention and the situation here was really about reinventing the wheel. After all, it was all about emphasising what we ought to have been doing anyway. So, every single procedure, every SoP, every rule was revisited. More importantly, it should all have been implemented as of yesterday. Such was the urgency felt which then translated into expediency of execution and implementation.

In 48 hours, the company was reinvented and best practices put into place. Even a story on how the accident occurred had to be invented. Accidental discharge of weapon due to negligence was not acceptable - heads would have rolled or someone's career could have been fixed, mine being the first in line.

The following Monday after the incident was the day of reckoning. It was literally the day my fate was to be decided that too that early into the tenure. Forces work in a unique fashion though. The first step is almost always taken to save people involved from long term ramifications of a punishment doled out. In many cases, unofficial punishment is meted out where the recipient appears repentant enough. Even before that, it is squarely established whether the mistake was due to an error of judgement or an error of intent. Errors of intent are almost in all cases met with an exemplary punishment. Once it is understood, evidence or not, that there has been just an error of judgement, it then becomes a case of whether or not the superiors want to fix the guy involved. The Court of inquiry then merely proceeds to find evidence in support of the decision taken.

Luckily, for me and my boss, we were thought of as 'good guys'. A rule was found and the need for the court of inquiry evaporated. My boss and I escaped the treatment that could have been otherwise.

"You must know what is really important as an officer in counter-terrorism environment in the valley", said my boss to me. "You have to learn to manage the environment."

"How do we define the environment, sir?", I naturally asked.

"The environment consists of anybody and everybody who is a stakeholder in this setup. The team of boys you lead, the *awam* (local population), the higher headquarters, the local politicians, the police machinery, the judicial machinery, each one of these is the environment", replied the boss.

"Yes sir", I acknowledged and added the boss' name to the environment.

However, the 'what ifs' remained. The biggest of all being "what if someone had accidentally gotten shot and a life was lost?" I, hence, decided to redraw my personal priorities. A new reality dawned upon me.

It was a team after all that I lead. And the best way to do well was to get the team to perform. It's one's own selflessness and sacrifice of the 'I' above all else that makes one a great leader. Thus, began an endeavour to excel at every aspect of command - morale of the boys above all else as a means to excel at command. Becoming a story could wait.

But morale is not so easily built. It is a function of confidence and belief in one's own and in this case one's team's abilities. And above all else, the team has to believe in the larger vision and purpose of the establishment. Confidence itself could be built through training but to excel at training, the personal administration and logistics also mattered. And of course, in an operational area, there are serious constraints around availability of people and time for training.

The company was heavily committed operationally. With internal road opening parties, area domination patrols and ambushes going out everyday, very few people were left even to carryout simple daily chores in the op base[4] with barely anyone available for guarding the base. The few guards who remained had to be relieved by the CHM[5] himself so that the guard could have his lunch at times. Such were the time commitments and to think of now finding time for training appeared to be a problem. But it had to be done!

Thus began a two pronged plan - one aimed at achieving higher operational standards through training and another aimed at achieving better standards of hygiene, sanitation and boarding and lodging within the base.

---

[4] The op base was defended as a safe haven out of which the soldiers operated and in which they rested when not out on operations.

[5] Company Havildar Major is a senior NCO responsible for the manpower, discipline and detailing for duties.

The later was quite easily done. I had manpower drawn from the Sikhs, Gorkhas and Jats under my command, for whom putting together resources is pretty easy. Sikhs are easily the most resourceful, they can practically bring you anything short of the moon (and on a clear night even that perhaps). One has to just ask. So, putting together wooden logs, cement, bajri, sand, tractors and even a road roller was easy. In the process, I also rediscovered the forgotten art of barter. After all, the only currency I had at disposal were the likes of fuel and rations that at times may become surplus. A Gorkha with his numerous skills can be a great artisan, carpenter, fabricator, et al besides being a great soldier. While at the same time a Jat will help keep the conscious alive with his great auditing skills while keeping a close frugal watch on movement of funds and materials.

The outcome was truly well received and if there were any doubts about what I was upto were soon dispelled. The op base was entirely refurbished. The men now had cleaner and more hygienic latrines to go to. The living areas were better ventilated, and equipped with cemented beds. The cook house and the mess were recreated. Lots of waste open space cleared and play grounds created. The base suddenly had playing facilities for Volleyball, Handball, and a mini football ground. The roads leading in to the base were levelled. New shelters were created including one for recreation. As also, a new refrigerator with soft drinks was commissioned. The base was now a happier place to live in.

The boys found things more convenient. They joyfully came back from work looking forward to a game of soccer. The energy in the camp was unbelievable. The faces no longer looked tired. It was amazing to see the vigour with which the boys played even after a long difficult day at work. Playing and sweating had a magical effect in the general happiness as also in the lowering of stress levels. This alone contributed to the turnaround in the company's mood after the accident. But the best was yet to come.

Implementing a well structured training was a lot trickier. The conventional training ideas were clearly not feasible. Training in the Army was always a well thought out short term exercise that required mobilisation of resources. The trainees and trainers would then be dedicated to the task for a duration of time sometimes upto a month. However, given the situation, this was not feasible. Manpower could not be spared even for an entire day for training. Such was the operational strain on manpower and resources. I had a difficult problem at hand. But then, I felt it was the key to survival and superior operational performance.

The CHM and the Senior JCO (SJ) were called in next by me to understand how the men would take to the idea of training in the op base. After all, it had never been done earlier. Anyone and everyone inducting into the op area was put through a pre-induction training at the higher headquarters before being posted to the companies. One also underwent a fifteen days induction training. But that was it. A soldier was now expected to use this fifteen days training over the rest of the tenure in the valley. And there was no provision for training alongside one's own team - the team a soldier was expected to operate with. Success at operations is largely a function of how well the team members understood each other as radio communication between each individual team member is not feasible.

The CHM and SJ were, therefore, suitably confused since the allocation of time was a concern. I then suggested that perhaps we have to rethink the way we traditionally trained. Rather than prolonged durations of only training, it would be better to think of training as an ongoing continuous process such that we train just two hours everyday. Each day the team going out for night time routine operations was given more than half the day off. Since each team would go out in rotation, it was decided that everyday between 10 AM and 12 noon, this team would undergo training conducted by respective team leaders.

As a result of this, each team trained twice a week. With the team finding these two hours to sit together and the team leader picking up a topic of choice, a large variety of topics would be discussed and drills practiced. Occasionally, the team would indulge in weapon cleaning and firing practice. Above all else, the team got sometime to sit and discuss operations. This was significantly important as this allowed team members to build non-verbal communication - the ability to understand each other without speaking a word. For a team of even ten people to be able to understand each other without speaking during night time operations was a major breakthrough. Sound carries real far at night and a spoken word heard by the enemy in the dead of the night could be the difference between success and failure of an operation. Such was the importance of communicating and understanding team dynamics in an operation.

Training began to yield excellent results in operations. The pride of the boys in their team grew and so did the confidence in their own abilities. Most importantly, training was able to focus their minds in the present - here and now and away from most distractions. Needless to say, with fewer distractions came fewer accidents. Life in the op base had changed sharply from before. There was a renewed positivity in the company with the incident long forgotten. Training alone had contributed beautifully to building newer, higher levels of morale.

The CHM was particularly happy. For every single person returning to the camp after a short absence on account of leave, temporary duty or anything else would spend the first three days training and as part of the CHM's team and not proceed to respective teams. This helped firstly refocus the returning soldier to the task at hand and not get pushed into active duty immediately. Additionally, this afforded the CHM a small team that could be employed at times for routine chores as also on activities for the upkeep and maintenance of the company area. Resultantly, the company was forever ready for any inspection even at short notice, such was the preparedness and the upkeep of the company area.

My personal directions and supervision for a couple of months had ensured that this new training routine had become a norm. There were numerous other changes to the norm. Leave planning was one such change.

Leave though a privilege for an army man, is nevertheless required to unwind and destress away from a war-zone. Being with the family also allows a soldier to discharge important obligations back home. Typically, in an army unit where an officer gets to spend substantial time with troops, the officer knows every single person under his command well or at least is supposed to.

In a RR[6] setup, things are different. RR draws its soldiers from a host of different units and typically the officers from another. This makes it difficult for a Company Commander to administer people, especially in areas where intimate previous knowledge about an individual is the key to taking sound decisions. Given the stress in a combat zone, it was no surprise then, that everyone wanted to avail maximum leave. It is not uncommon for men to lie and come up with all kinds of excuses to avail leave.

Grant of leave is also a powerful tool in the hands of the CoCo and the SJ. But the CoCo's decision on whom to grant leave to and whom not to, can have a huge impact on the morale of the boys. Since, sneaking on your team mates is not considered ethical, men generally would not inform anyone when someone is lying even if they knew. Hence,

---

[6] Rashtriya Rifles is a set up under the Home ministry that was specifically raised for counter-terrorism operations in the Kashmir Valley and draws its manpower from various Army units.

granting leave to a liar would severely affect the boys. Worse was the reverse, when I was unable to grant leave to a truly deserving candidate. To obviate this, invariably I had to relent to a good reason for leave. But deciding who should be allowed to proceed on leave could be stressful in a combat zone. After all, the routine duties had to be performed and I had to be prepared for contingencies. A depleted op base especially due to excessive leaves is never a good thing.

To overcome the dilemma, I decided to democratise the leave management. The SJ was immediately up in arms. He felt this would severely undermine his power in the organisation. Thankfully for me, this was not a corporate organisation. After a little bit of trying to reason it out with the SJ, I simply passed an order that it be done. The SJ was pacified with the words that let's give it a try. Giving him a small emergency quota helped the situation.

Hence, it was decided that the decision who proceeds on leave will be henceforth, taken by the team itself. The minimum manpower required to run the operation's base was calculated and barring a little extra for unforeseen requirements, it was decided that the rest of the number could be on leave. Thus, platoon wise quotas were worked out and leave quotas shared with the Platoons Havildars. Now at every time, not more than the number authorised were allowed to be on leave. I had expressly conveyed that I was not interested in deciding who proceeds on leave and for what reason. I now only had to be told that one of the boys had returned from leave and another was ready to proceed in his place. Incidentally, the lying totally stopped now. Since one could no longer lie to one's own friends who also came from the same area as him.

When in field, the time spent in travelling between the op base and the transit camps is considered to be on duty. Surprisingly, the peer pressure now was such that boys took minimum time in transit as invariably a close friend of his, who was due to leave next, was breathing down on the returning soldier's neck and keeping track of his movement. This too improved the availability of manpower in the op base.

Boys were also used to collecting food from the mess and then reheating the same in their living areas before consumption. This is quite an important activity as the men who are part of a team, bond with each other over a meal. In the field, firstly there was no opportunity to indulge in such activities. But more importantly, it was a potential hazard given the fact that men slept in the barracks alongside their weapons and ammunition. A fire mishap could have major repercussions.

I decided that it was important to put an end to this. However, cold food was a big morale dampener. Hence, I undertook to improve the cook house and langar. Food once cooked would obviously start to go cold, especially in a place like Kashmir. Since, it was assumed that the men would collect food and then proceed to give it their own trademark 'tadka', the quality could just about be fine and nothing more. Lastly, there really was no proper and adequate place for the boys to sit and eat.

The issue needed redressal at multiple levels. To start with, the food quality had to be brought to the mark where no-one felt the need to reheat food or even tinker with the flavour. The cookhouse staff was accordingly set right. They were no longer allowed to reheat their own food and were required to eat out of the food already cooked. This lead to a 50% improvement in food quality immediately. Next was the issue of food being kept hot for consumption since men were used to eating the major meals over a one hour window. I launched a study into the assets of the company to find that we were already in possession of a food warmer. It had, however, never been put to use, no one knew since when. With a little cleaning and maintenance, the food warmer was brought in near perfect shape.

The third problem of adequate sitting space was very easily addressed. The Gorkha boys created a cosy little hut right next to the cookhouse, complete with sitting spaces and a Bukhari for the winters. It actually became the preferred place to dine for the men. As an added advantage, there was now lesser wastage of food as being able to take what one wanted to eat multiple times, became a possibility. This reduced food related litter in the op base. Now, eating together had a new meaning.

To realise that most things were now taken care of, I could take a sigh of relief. Seeing the improvements in the op base, the Commanding Officer (CO) too pitched in with some material help and release of two new shelters. I too had a new room to live out of and the luxury of running water in the attached rest room. The shelter came with an adjoining room built out of pre-fabricated materials. The shift out of the previous room made me lonelier as I parted ways with the mouse that lived with me and often greeted me in the mornings, perched on top of the very sleeping bag I would pop out of. The mouse did get new company in the old room though.

One of the highlights of the time was the arrival of a top class officers' mess chef in the company. This highly trained cook (who had received training in a couple of 5 star hotels sponsored by his parent unit) was sent on a punishment posting as he had an unfortunate altercation in his parent unit with his CO. Unknown to the Bn HQ[7], he cleared all filters to eventually reach the company. The men from his parent unit quickly brought to my notice his great culinary skills. What followed was an unexpected gluttony of epic proportions. Everyone was happy to be enjoying better cooked meals. I was especially happy since occasionally I would get to eat Chinese and Continental food. This was not to continue for long though. As the Bn 2IC learnt of this soon on one of his visits to the company. The next time the cook was returning from leave, he was conveniently retained in the officers' mess. I was now back to eating the regular dal and subzi, missing the occasional break in monotony.

Mandir parades exist in peacetime stations and are rarely seen in areas such as where the company was deployed. However, I decided to ensure that regular

---

[7] Battalion Headquarter - Six companies of the kind the CoCo commanded came together to form a battalion.

mandir parades are organised on every Tuesday, in keeping with the traditions of the Army in peacetime and the term 'parade'. From within the men, a soldier who was a stout believer of Lord Shiva was chosen to be the equivalent of the company priest. Now every Tuesday evening, the boys would indulge in an energetic mandir parade, engaging in singing bhajans. Occasionally, the bhakts would indulge in dancing to bhajans of Lord Krishna in an almost trance like state. The weekly mandir parades had an amazing impact on soothing the nerves of the boys. More importantly, it kept men hopeful in the blessings of the Gods.

Incidentally, one side of the op base was a water reservoir meant for irrigation purposes. While the locals used the waters for growing paddy, for the company it was a boon. Firstly, the water table was at three feet. Secondly, and more importantly, it had fishes in it. In the summers, as the fishes came closer to the surface, the Gurkhas could be seen laying suitable baits to catch the fish. It was invariably the duty of the guard from the platoon to look after the fishes so caught, duly marinated and left to dry on the fence. When the men returned in the evening, they would cook the same and enjoy the bounties of nature. Every once in a while, especially on days when I would spot the marinated fishes left to dry on the fence during the daytime round of the base, I too would receive a well cooked fish alongside the evening dinner from the platoon. I for long wondered if this was their love for me or a simple bribe to let the fishing continue. In return, I would send across a 1 litre bottle of a soft drink. That was gratitude for sure.

Simultaneously, a number of other issues and processes were streamlined. As the new routine and processes cemented their way towards permanency and the new normal, I began to feel more relaxed and confident in the abilities of the company. It was time now to rededicate to a focus on matters external to the company.

Understanding the environment

In the meantime, the world outside the op base continued to evolve and fast. The environment was also looking for opportunities to size me up - the new CoCo. There hadn't been any real situation thus far. I had mostly familiarised with the terrain and then sorted out the administrative and logistic issues within the op base.

For the people within my area of responsibility and generally entire Kashmir, it had been nearly 16 years since the local situation turned disturbed and insurgency really started. So, if anyone who needed to mature and come to an understanding of the local environment, it was me.

The standard tenure for most men and Company Commanders in Kashmir lasted 30 months. Anyone, who designed the thirty months tenure was a genius. For it typically took six months to come to terms with the assignment, another one year of hard work to understand the situation and the last one year to deliver any real results. After that, a soldier is practically tired and needs to be turned over. However, the Kashmiri had been there forever and in the process seen many a soldier come and go. The locals knew the system better and better still, they were well adapted and some even knew how to milk the system.

The survival of the militants depended entirely on the support of the local population - if not everyone then at least a few of them. Conversely, seeking these militants out also required help of the local population. The point is - help is not always voluntarily forthcoming. The militants stay within the population and operate out of it. The Armed forces on the other hand have to operate from a distance while building those bridges with the population. No one wants bad hats to thrive and grow within the society. But, finally it is the economics of it all that drives actions. Provisioning for the demands of the militants could be a rather profitable business. And those who are able to bridge the gap to their trust, are able to indirectly wield the power of the gun without having to carry a weapon. They even controlled the government machinery by eliminating those who did not support their cause. But not everyone can be happy, though they could be afraid. Getting quality information takes a lot more. I was to learn in due course of time.

As of now, it was still early days. I had to make do with what I had been told. The gyan sessions during the interactions at the transit camps on induction served as a good baseline to start with. And thus began phase I of my mission - 'find the militants'.

The plan was simple - meet everyone who lives in the area - sarpanches, government officials, police representatives, party workers, known/suspected sympathisers, surrendered terrorists, etc - which was practically everyone living in the area. The average estimate of population in the area was approximately 20,000 people in all. Reaching out and establishing a line of communication with each one of them was important. I had to literally go house to house meeting people in an attempt to better understand the dynamics in the area but more importantly to build an impression of being nice and approachable. In the process, I came across a wide variety of people. Some of these seeing an opportunity to get close to the new Company Commander start talking. People have varied agendas. I unsuspectingly succumbed to a few. After all, I was still learning.

The first kind of people who start talking are the history tellers. These are people who are quite well placed and wanted to remain aloof in the entire play of things but being better groomed also wished to impress upon me - a new comer, with their knowledge and upbringing. So, they would narrate tales from the recent past - tales of past actions, stories of what past Company Commanders did, stories of episodes that they felt were narratable. These were stories that were interesting and only contributed towards understanding the present. Of not much tactical value but good to learn of certain do's and don't's to be kept in mind - for only the most impressionable stories were remembered and retold. I thus learnt what left a lasting impression. Almost no-one talked about it, but most incidents that are retold are the ones that are also the most painful. And the pain was for me to figure out.

The valley in 2004 was well past the worst in terms of militancy. The few militants who remained were rather hard core. Gone were the days of heavy engagements with a large number of militants. The engagements had to be precise and swift now. The number of engagements too had dropped significantly. The drop in militant numbers had given rise to a political form of militancy - whereby the militants avoided any direct engagement with the Army but on the contrary activated the local population to indulge in trouble making through strikes, road blocks, protest marches, etc.

However, and thankfully, the conscience of the population as a whole was alive with a clear sense of justice, at least when on the receiving end. The general population appreciated just and upright government officials and I saw myself as a representative of the Hindu majority of India in a Muslim majority neighbourhood in Kashmir. The standards expected were therefore, of the highest order. It was also a choice for a Company Commander to be just & upright or to be a tyrant with just one focus on delivering the results. Making the choice was not as easy though. Circumstances played a vital role in pushing anyone to choose a way going forward. Pressures created by the peer group and the seniors played a major role too. But, finally it boiled down to who I chose to be and the amount of pressure (generally self inflicted) that I feel I could handle.

"Just the way one cannot treat fire with fire - tyranny does not work - more so when the law and order machinery is robust and mass media coverage intensive. On the contrary a humane, approachable nature builds trust and goodwill. But is that enough to succeed with the local population? Only time would tell.", I thought contemplating the way forward.

In the meantime, there was work to be done. For ease of operations planning & execution, I had to familiarise with every inch of the terrain under my area of responsibility. I was yet to engage with every house, in every mohalla of every village personally. Every stakeholder - government officials with work related responsibilities in the area were to be met with and understood. I had to meet every one in the immediate neighbourhood, especially the other neighbouring Company Commanders. Every business related interest in the area, well even the animals had to be mapped and their operating patterns understood. And while on that note, there were fair bit of wild animals too - leopards, tigers and bears that would come down to the valley floor at night especially during winters. Leopards were shy of human beings but bears were not. God help you if a bear is headed your way and you can't get out of the way. In many cases, one would end up being slapped by the bear. It could be especially dangerous if the claws catch you and not the entire palm. The night vision devices came in handy in such cases. After all forewarned is forearmed.

Thus, I began aggressive patrolling of the areas by day and night. Daytime patrolling was more of an area familiarisation routine including meeting the local population. I met all the prominent people in the villages, conducting limited cordon and search operations in villages and search and destroy operations in the jungles. Both villages and jungles in Kashmir were peculiar in their own way.

Villages in Kashmir were built unlike villages in many other states of India. Here no two houses shared a common wall. Each house is an independent unit built within a small compound. The compound is fenced on all sides. The fencing in 99% of the houses is done with CGI roofing sheets. In many cases, these are the ones that were removed from the roofs the last time the roofs were fixed for leaking. The house roofs are slanting with adequate attic like space below them. One corner of the compound has a small 'koterie' for keeping animals which also doubles up as a store for firewood. Winters in Kashmir are wet and cold. In another corner, you could find another cubicle structure raised well above the ground on stilts used as a toilet of sorts. Below the toilet, one could invariably find a heap of human faeces. It was not uncommon for women of the house to clear the shit and carry it on their heads to the fields nearby for disposal. Kashmiri women are beautiful. But every once in a while, you would come across one on the road carrying this stink. That one moment could present quite an experience in contrast.

Most houses do not possess any furniture at all. The floors are lined with wall to wall carpeting. Inside the house, everyone moves barefoot. The carpeted floor is used for sitting or sleeping on. Kashmiri villagers in general followed a minimalist approach to living. At an average, most members of the family survived on 2-3 pairs of clothing and a pair of slippers/shoes each. Above the clothes, almost everyone wore a complete coverall called a 'firan'. The firan covers it all and is used except in peak summer months when the firans get a good wash and some rest. The beauty of the firan is such that it can be used to form a good heat trap which is especially useful in winters.

The menfolk and the elderly get to carry a wood coal powered heater called the 'kangri' inside the firans in the winters. This allowed the men folk to venture out in winters and brave the cold. With not much work to do, all some then had to do was to sit huddled together and gossip. The womenfolk had to either brave the cold or use the warmth of the hearth in the house. The aged, elderly women carried the coal kangdi too.

From the security forces perspective, the firan was a risk for it concealed too much. It could allow a negative element the luxury of sneaking up a weapon to close proximity of the security forces. Thus, a comforting piece of clothing for the Kashmiri was a discomforting one for the security forces. Whenever a military patrol approached the locals, it was standard practice to lift one's firan so that it became clear the local is unarmed. However, it always broke the heat trap inside and was a pain for the locals. But for the purposes of security, this had to be done.

The houses were all built on a raised plinth that was at least two feet above the ground level, perhaps to cater to the snow in the winters. Most houses used a guinea bag at the entrance for a foot mat. Some would use more than one. Most houses followed a simple standard interior architecture. The entrance was almost always in the middle leading to a passage with doors on either side leading to the rooms. In case of more than one floor, a staircase from the passage would lead to the upper floors or the attic in case of just one floor. In one of the rooms towards the back away from the main entrance, would be the kitchen. Many kitchens still used wood as a fuel whereas a few, who could pay for it, used LPG for cooking.

Like in most parts of the country, the quality of living was a clear indicator of the economic status of the family. Most families kept away from exhibiting their true earnings to keep attempts of extortion at bay. Most houses in the villages stole electric power illegally while only the richest and most effluent had a legal electric connection that was metered. Nearly no one in the villages, owned a car and if at all anyone did, it was around the Maruti 800 variety. Mid segment sedans and upper segment cars and SUVs were difficult to find. Interestingly, most cars had a Delhi registration number on it. Bringing in second hand cars from Delhi for resale in Kashmir, was a great business.

All villages had a small area typically on the main road passing next to the village where a small market of sorts thrived. The size of the market was proportionate to the size of the village it serviced. The market typically catered to small needs - baked bread (commonly called double roti) being the most important of all for it was invariably used for breakfast by most households along with tea. Apparently, people did not like to cook in the mornings. Besides, a meat shop, a grocery shop, a tailor shop were regular features in most such markets. For the major purchases, one had to venture into the nearest town.

Handwara or Handwor as the locals called it was the nearest large town. It is an important town where roads from Baramulla[8] to the South, Sopore[9] to the East, Drugmulla (and Kupwara) to the North and a road going deeper into the hinterland to the West intersected. This is where the headquarters of perhaps one of the longest continuously stationed RR battalions in the valley was located. The roads leading to the West lead into the Rajwar forest that ran parallel to the LOC[10] with a section longitudinally jutting Eastwards towards Handwara. The forest was quite thick to suit anyone who wanted to hide and additionally was long and deep enough to facilitate undetected cross movement. No wonder, it was a favourite

---

[8] known as Varahamula in antiquity.

[9] known as Suyyapur in antiquity and nicknamed as Chhotta London for its prosperity at one point in time.

[10] Line of control with Pakistan

of the terrorists since the very beginning. Legend has it that in the 1990s, nearly 250 terrorists inhabited the forest drawing a substantial chunk from across the borders from areas as far away as Afghanistan. Stories of ferocious gun battles between these and security forces were still rife. Incidentally, before the security forces deployed in the CI grid system in the mid 90s, these terrorists roamed around in large numbers in the open. The very ground where I had my company base located then, was the venue for a mini cricket league between the terrorist teams until a few years before.

Adjoining the Rajwar forest to the North was the Haphruda forest. An even more dreaded forest in the area but not as infested. Perhaps the higher altitude had something to do with it or was it because of the Sikhs deployed there. Nevertheless, that too was used extensively by the terrorists for transiting between various sectors and areas. It was commonplace to see trees marked with arrows pointing in the direction of major cities and towns around. The militants used these as guiding marks. The militants preferred to live out of forests that were on the fringes of villages and did not require a lot of climbing. They created good hideouts within the forests sometimes. Typically, militant hideouts would lie midway from the bottom to the top on a slope away from well known tracks and paths. The hideouts were dug into the ground three to four feet below the surface. The tops would have temporary roofs made out of wooden logs covered with waterproof linings made of tarpaulin or plastic sheets which were in turn covered with mud and revegetated. Some of these hideouts could be as large as a small 8'x8' room and in some cases just foxholes, enough to host one or two person(s). The deadliest were of course complexes with large hideouts in the middle and foxholes all around.

However, now a good ten to fifteen years down the line, things were very different. A handful of militants remained. As per Army estimates then, a total of 700-800 militants in all operated in Kashmir. Most others had either surrendered or had perished with time. However, only the fittest remained per Darwin's theory. The smaller number also meant lower concentration. Even the militants were very careful and avoided mistakes that other's had made in the past. Some Kashmiri militants had survived in the system for as long as 7 to 8 years.

One such militant was Md. Ayub Khan - a terrorist who had been operating for more that nine years then. Over the previous nine years, many of his colleagues had perished. While he had grown to become the head of Hizbul Mujahideen in North Kashmir as well as the Finance Head - the man charged with the onerous task of raising money to sustain the operations of the terrorist group. He was considered to be an amicable terrorist, not the usual terror type terrorist, who was well enmeshed into the lives of the local Kashmiris. He also acted as a conduit to spread their ideology. The mere fact that he had survived for nine long years spoke about his survival skills and unfortunately, his popularity as well.

"Get him and you will get the Kirti Chakra for sure", the Commanding Officer had said to me during his induction briefing.

While looking to sanitise the area of militant activities, special emphasis was therefore on Ayub. But Ayub was known to operate in the adjoining areas and almost never visited my area.

The only way to reach a militant was through the informers. However, selection of informers and cultivating them is a tricky business. Firstly, it is impossible to know who is going to help you in the first place. For an informer, it is risky business. Risk might mean putting one's life in danger. But then life is in danger even if one is generally starving or worse still - leading a meaningless life - a sort of midlife crisis. In other cases, enmity or past history leading to hatred could drive an individual into becoming an informer. Finding an informer, therefore, entailed first finding a sympathiser. Finding a sympathiser was relatively easier. A lot of people were generally ready to point towards a sympathiser of the militants (also called an over ground worker or OGW for short) since the OGW does not carry a gun but wields the power of the gun indirectly. People in general hate an OGW for this indirect derived power that an OGW flaunts. Additionally, since a large part of the population is pointing at an OGW, it is difficult for the terrorists to single any one person out to be blamed for blowing the OGW's cover. Dealing with too many could cause erosion of the so called popular base for the terrorists.

Once identified, it was easy for me to show a general, above average interest in the OGW and his activities. A few interactions arouse the interest of the OGW's enemies or detractors - invariably a troubled neighbour. After that, it's just about building a communication channel. Thankfully, telecom companies had just about been permitted to operate in the valley and people had taken to the available Airtel and BSNL connections rather quickly. I had my own number advertised all over the area for anyone to call in. The phone calls were yet to come though, since the telephone penetration was still low. This was fast changing though. Mobile phones were fast catching the imagination of the youth and everyone wanted one, especially the youngsters. It allowed them to remain in touch with each other. A sure relief from the night curfews.

Mobile phones were thus the new incentive. There were more takers for 'lob a grenade, get Rs. 5000 scheme' floated by terrorists. It was also a great deal for the terrorists who could continue to remain hidden, while keeping the issue alive through occasional grenade blasts. It's virtually impossible to nab an unknown face with no prior history of crime in a crowded area who had just lobbed a grenade and disappeared in the ensuing melee. Peer pressure could kill.

The administration maintained a standing force of 'ikhwanis' that comprised of surrendered militants. They had no clear organisation of their own, hence, they worked in small groups with the Army units. Ten years into the militancy problem in Kashmir, a large number of local terrorists, seeing an evident negative outcome of the war waged on the state, had become reasonably disillusioned with the so called 'freedom movement' and an armed struggle in Kashmir. As a result, a large number had surrendered and looked forward to a normal life. Many had sought to be re-integrated into the society. Most had joined the territorial army - the ikhwani unit of surrendered militants. It correctly used the skills acquired by them as part of militant training. A large platoon of these men was stationed at Handwara.

I was out on a liaison visit to Handwara and happened to meet a few of these ikhwanis in the office complex. The ikhwanis like most Kashmiris had a natural better lung capacity, having been brought up in the higher altitudes in Kashmir. Additionally, perhaps because of their training, they were well built and muscular. The question was whether they could be trusted. Although well versed with the ways of the militants, there was very little intelligence forthcoming from them. With such a backdrop of information, I met the ikhwanis and the usual pleasantries followed.

"Sir! I know a lot of people in your area. I come from village Woskura in your area. I will help you with useful information on terrorist movements in your area.", said Ishaq, one of the ikhwanis. Ishaq was in his early 40s and had joined the Hizbul Mujahiddin in his 20s. He had seen militancy develop from its very early days. Coming from a reasonably well to do middle class family, he had picked up the weapon because it was pretty fashionable then. His closest friends had all joined along with him, for various reasons. Some because of the lure of 'the power of the gun', some 'simply because his friend was doing it too' and many just wanted to make a fashion statement then.

A close friend circle of ten had enjoyed an eventful and adventurous outing with the militant group in its heydays. Now only four remained of the original group, the others had been eliminated in various contacts with the security forces. The job was no longer glamorous enough when the remaining four friends decided to quit and surrender, taking an olive branch extended by the government in Kashmir. The group or what was left of it was no longer as jovial as it used to be once. The unmindful exuberance of the youth was replaced with the seriousness that middle age brings as also the realisation of all they had done.

The others in the group had remained quiet and appeared to be blank. I exchanged my mobile number with the group and left. The same evening I received a call.

"Is that Maqbool Saheb?", said the deep voice on the other end.

"Yes. It is!", I said, acknowledging my pseudo name. It was customary for the military personal to conceal their real identity in the operational area. There had been many frivolous and fake registrations of human rights cases against key defence personal with the objective of slowing them down. The fake identity did not hide crimes but definitely provided some relief from concerted efforts at the behest of the militants to implicate military leadership.

"I was at the meeting this afternoon. I am Riyaz.", said the voice - an ikhwani. There was a certain confidence yet a tinge of foreboding in the voice that I could sense. It was the voice of a person who had been in suffering for long and had been sad at the heart.

"I liked meeting you today. I would like to meet you again.", said Riyaz. "But the meeting has to be a secret."

"Sure! I can meet you. Where would you like to meet?", I said.

"You come towards Bakiakar village, I will meet you at the table top behind the village towards the forest at 4PM.", Riyaz replied.

"OK", I said and hung up. I got thinking. "The route to the meeting point passed through the forest. Could this be a trap?", my training was talking to me. "But the meeting had to be honoured." I had to keep my word.

A plan was formed. Two teams moved out simultaneously towards the forest. The plan was to take two different but adjoining routes. If any of the routes was trapped or worse ambushed at least the other team could provide immediate backup. My team would proceed for the meeting and the backup team could then return to the base like any normal patrol. The beefed up strength would also be a deterrent for any foul play.

Fortunately, there wasn't any. I was laughing at my immaturity. Terrorists would generally not do anything spectacular inside a forest where they would not even get public attention. I was not yet a target important enough for the terrorists to get rid off.

When I reached the meeting point, Riyaz was already there, waiting for me.

"Jai Hind Saheb!", said Riyaz after the customary frisking by the scouts. The frisking was a standard procedure followed by the lead scouts.

"Jai Hind!", I returned the salutation. It felt strange to hear those words from a Kashmiri. It was rare. Not even officials in the civil government machinery used this form of salutation. Riyaz was either a patriot or an imposter. Only time would tell.

I and Riyaz settled for a little conversation. The rest of the team moved away and occupied all round defence with me in the middle, ensuring no one can get through and disturb the meeting and more importantly spot the person I was meeting with.

"Sir! I am from Bakiakar village. I had crossed over along with many others in 1995. Most of those you met the other day had crossed over around the same time. We came back with some training and a gun. Life was good. Everyone respected us. But we were required to create a lot of trouble then. Do anything that caught media attention. But very soon the charm of being a militant began to fade away. We were required to be subservient to the Pak and Afghan terrorists. They gave us orders and we were required to carry them out. In many cases, killing our own Kashmiri brethren who showed any dissent against us. Inspite of all we did, they never trusted us. It just did not feel like a freedom struggle. Then the Army came in and many of our friends were killed. So, when the Army extended an olive branch asking us to surrender, many of us did in 2001.", Riyaz began to open his heart out.

"Now things are different. There are very few militants who remain and most are from across. They belong to militant tanzims like Lashkar-e-Taiba (LeT), Harkat-ul-Jihadi-Islami (HuJI), Harkat-ul-Mujahideen (HuM), very few militants are from Kashmir and those belong to Hizbul Mujahideen (HM). Most foreign militants are unable to converse with the locals and find it difficult to understand Kashmiri language. Hence, for them to operate, they need local HM militants along. Furthermore, the handlers across are wary that HM militants may surrender. Besides the loss of a fighting trained militant, a gun and ammunition is also lost. For them, the gun is more important. As long as they have the gun, they will find someone to use it to their benefit. The lure of power and some quick money can do that.", continued Riyaz. It was almost as if Riyaz was talking to himself and contemplating his own life story thus far.

"But life now is still uncertain. I cannot sleep and spend a night in my own village. Surrendering is not acceptable to the handlers across. It sends a wrong signal. To ensure that no one else can take the step, they need to set an example. So, now, many like me are safe from the Indian Army and the police but not from the militants and their supporters- some of them my own people. The supporters are the best off in the scheme of things. They wield the real power without even lifting the gun. And they even get paid for it. The only way I can return to my village and to my people and lead a normal life is when every single militant is finished - dead or surrendered. Until then I have to be very careful and live like a homeless.", finished Riyaz gazing in the distance.

There was a distinct silence that lasted a few seconds but felt much longer. I continued to look at Riyaz hoping that he would continue. I had been a good listener and was enjoying coming upto speed with local history. Observing Riyaz in a pensive mood, I chose to very reluctantly disturb him.

"Riyaz! I am sure you have not called me here to tell me about the story of Kashmir in recent times.", I said. "So, why don't we get to the point?"

"Oh yes! I sometimes get carried away with all this. There are not many people I can talk to about this." Riyaz observed. "Actually I heard everything you said to the ikhwani group the other day. I did not wish to say anything then. But I want to help you as best as I can. Lots of people have already said the other day that they would help but you need to be careful. Not everything is the way it seems. Kashmir is a difficult place to live in and for most it is an everyday battle for survival."

"What should I be looking out for?", I asked, least expecting to hear what I had just done. Riyaz and the other ikhwanis had turned to militancy together and operated together for many years. One would thus expect such a cohesive group to be thick together. I did not know who to believe - the rest of the ikhwanis who seemed to have no such apprehensions but were openly willing to help or

Riyaz who had initially remained silent. I did know of course that time would tell.

"I sense you are new to the system. I only want you to be careful with people here. Not every thing is the way it seems. Do not trust people blindly.", said Riyaz once again.

"In fact, why don't you tell me who are you looking for? Your area of responsibility does not have any permanent operating terrorists. In fact, there is only one known terrorist from amongst the villages in your area and he is known to have not come back from across. No one knows if he is even alive. Your area is used as a transit area mostly. It is ideally located in the middle of major concentration areas. Your area is approximately two nights of walking distance from the LoC. Terrorists having infiltrated reach and cross your area in the third night and head to their areas of operations deeper in the valley. In other cases, it is at the cross roads of other higher concentration areas such as Rajwar forest to the South West, Hafruda forest to the North West, Lolab valley to the North East and Sopore belt to the South East. Terrorists do not operate or stay for long in your area. If at all, some may chose to stay a day or two. Hence, for you to strike you will have to be either lucky or receive real time information about their presence.", continued Riyaz.

Well at least this part Riyaz knew well and corroborated with my military appreciation. In my area of responsibility, there were no real deep forests for militants to operate out of for long, especially the foreign militants who preferred to usually stay outside the villages.

"Is there anyone you are specifically looking for? Mohd Ayub Khan?", asked Riyaz while I was still thinking.

Taken aback, I asked, "How did you know I was looking for him?"

"Well! Everyone of the military establishment is looking for him. So, naturally must also be you.", replied Riyaz.

"If you know so much, why don't you help?", I said.

"Ayub mostly operates between the Sopore-Baramulla-Kupwara triangle. He personally belongs to Kupwara. But he spends a lot of his time in the area South of Handwara, Langate. I know some people close to him as I have operated with them in the past. He is as much looking for my head as I am for his. When I hear of him, I will surely inform you.", said Riyaz. "As of now I should be leaving."

"But I thought it is only now we seem to be getting somewhere with this conversation.", I protested.

"You see Maqbool Saheb! I have to get out of my village and reach my destination for the night. It's going to be dark soon and I can't stay here.", clarified Riyaz. "But we will meet again soon."

I had no means of holding him back. His life was important too. And it was too early to host Riyaz in my own op base for the night. So, I said the customary goodbyes to Riyaz and began the trek back to the base. I had developed a soft corner for Riyaz already and sympathised with his condition.

The other team had already sanitised the area ahead. Hence, it was a quick walk back. On another day, I would have taken another route through my area but not today. My mind was too preoccupied with the interaction with Riyaz. The two hour long conversation with Riyaz had given me a perspective on my area of responsibility. Yes, the focus had to be on the transiting militants which meant developing a grid of information sources who would act as my eyes and ears on the ground. This would also mean simultaneously making it difficult for the militants to cross over through the area or at least upsetting their time plans.

I had barely entered my op base when my phone began to ring again. This time it was Ishaq from the ikhwani group I had met earlier.

"Maqbool Saheb! It's me Ishaq. We have information about a confirmed OGW from village Gyanpora. He is in confirmed possession of a cache of arms and ammunition. Very difficult to normally find, he is right now in his house. We are reaching in fifteen minutes. Let's go and pick him up for interrogation.", said the voice. I had barely said OK when Ishaq hung up the phone. I was excited. My visit to the Ikhwanis was already yielding positive results.

Though, it was 6.45 PM and getting dark, I hastily put together a team of eight boys from amongst the reserves. The guard at the gate had been instructed to flag down a civil vehicle for travelling in a military vehicle this late would have been a giveaway. The village mentioned was in the area of responsibility of the neighbouring company commander. But the lack of any action in a long time got my adrenaline kicking in to take the risk without any mandatory approvals.

"So what if the neighbouring company commander is senior? I have actionable information. I will inform him and the boss later. Let's get it done first. The boss will be happy after all.", I thought.

Things were moving so fast that before I realised, I was already at the wheel of the impounded Tata Sumo with my team and the ikhwanis hurtling down towards village Gyanpora. The Sumo had of course been procured by emptying out a shuttle between Handwara and Magam passing through the op base location. There were a few protests by the commuters but when they realised the urgency with which the team was moving, they had no choice but to shut up and wait for the vehicle to return or catch alternative modes of transport which were nearly none at the late hour for a general curfew existed in the area after dark.

The village happened to be on the internal road and I knew the only Checkpost on the road was my own. With no traffic on the road, the vehicle reached the village in fifteen minutes. I could drive fast, being from the Armoured Corps helped. The team was briefed on the way. The other ikhwani accompanying Ishaq was also introduced but I was hardly listening. The boys were briefed to spend minimum time in the village as we planned to extricate before anyone could react.

The house of the target was on the main road itself. In less than 5 minutes, the target was identified, apprehended and put into the vehicle and the return journey began. The return journey was even shorter.

The whole episode was over in less than an hour. On reaching the op base, Ishaq literally instructed me as an experienced hand would treat a novice, "It's already quite late, you extract the information from him as to where has he hidden the arms. We will see you in the morning.", with that the ikhwanis left.

I did not want to appear clueless as to how does one extract information for I really had no idea having never done it earlier. This is when all those interactions in the transit camps began to come back to me. I was now smiling, a smile of relief that after all I did know or so I thought.

With the ikhwanis leaving, there was a sudden void. Everything was suddenly very quiet. Barring the guards on the target, even the team had been dismissed. I was thinking hard about how to get the whereabouts of the cache out of the target. "Should I start with simple questioning or use third degree straightaway? Would I appear too soft? Should I call some of our heftier boys to sort of soften him up first?", I was busy thinking.

Just then the Signalman came running outside and said to me, "Haider is on the line and wants to speak with you urgently." Haider was the boss's pseudo name. It was uncharacteristic for him to call at this hour. He typically called a little later for an update on the day's developments and plans for the next day. And additionally, he was already holding the line waiting for me as against the usual message to call back. Something was amiss.

"Maqbool for Haider. Good evening sir!", I said coming on the line.

"Maqbool! I want you to immediately check if any Tata Sumo has crossed your Checkpost with people dressed in military uniform inside. They have picked up an individual from village Gyanpora in your neighbouring area. If not, be on the look out and stop them from crossing. I want to know what is going on. Check immediately and report back.", Haider directed and hung up. He appeared disturbed on the call.

I knew instantly things had gone wrong. I had gone beyond my area that too in the dark without informing anyone. The villagers had soon after the apprehension gathered as a mass and with lit torches marched to the local company op base who had in turn called up the boss. The people were acting in time to save one of their kin. There had been a few claimed disappearances already in the past. Of course, I had not anticipated this. Thankfully, in the dark owing to the swiftness of the action, no one knew who had picked up the target. For me, it was cover up time now.

I called the boss back.

"Maqbool for Haider! We have stopped the vehicle and managed to get the gentleman off. He is with us now in the op base.", I said.

"Good! Look after him. It is quite dark now. I will talk to you in the morning." Haider hung up.

I had no idea what would have happened if Haider had asked about the identity of the people who had apprehended the target. Or is it that he had already guessed what had happened. It had been a rather hectic day. I now had a night to figure out what story to tell and gather my wits. Thankfully, no one was coming to me that night.

I ordered that the target be kept in isolation in a separate room under observation and be served with dinner. I had other things to look into. I quickly addressed and dispersed my team leaders with directions for the next day. People coming into and those going out of the op base had to be interviewed. Office letters needed to be drafted, vetted and signed for dispatch. Incoming official letters needed to be read and instructions given for dissemination. A host of other documentation needed to be completed. It was turning out to be a rather busy evening or was I trying to delay getting into the interrogation?

Soon after, I changed and freshened up and had a quick dinner. It was now finally time to solve the mystery that the target was. I had never done anything of the kind earlier. Techniques of interrogation were least known to me and I had to figure it out by myself. Third degree was definitely out of question. It was a terrible idea given the situation. It was already 9.30 PM. I knew that the target had had dinner an hour earlier. Probably, the target would be asleep by now, I half hoped. But the conversation had to happen. I was too anxious to wait until the morning.

To my surprise, the target was wide awake and sitting up in the room looking calm. He appeared rather confident for someone who had been apprehended in the manner that he was.

"I am surprised you are not asleep already.", I said to the target.

"Saheb! How can I sleep after having been brought here like this. Besides, I was sure I cannot be allowed to rest till you have spoken to me. So far, you have not said a word to me.", said the target.

"Actually, there is hardly anything I have to say. If anything you have to tell me why would you become a case of interest.", I was trying to sound tough.

"Sir! I am a poor man. I own an apple orchard and mostly stick to my business of growing and selling apples. The larger traders from Sopore contract our farms each year. That is about the maximum extent of my reach."

"I was hoping to hear your name first.", I said.

"I am sorry! I am Mohd Ilyas Bhat from village Gyanpora. I assumed you would know my name.", said the target. "I have no idea why I have been apprehended."

"Well! The people who had you apprehended will be back in the morning. And the truth will be known.", I said. "Unless you would want to come clean by yourself and make things easier for all of us".

"I too am hopeful that the truth will be out tomorrow. I have seen this situation for the last 15 years. A lot of people have been reported doing something wrong in the past and later they are found innocent.", said Ilyas.

"There is no smoke without fire. Why would people, who are also Kashmiri, complaint about another?", I asked.

"It happens all the time Saheb! In many cases it is simply personal enmity. A property dispute, someone can implicate you. A girl likes you, you can get implicated. Your family is doing well financially, someone jealous could implicate you. Such allegations are also used to pressurise one into subjugation. People who are close to the militants also do it often and in some cases, those close to the Army can also misuse proximity. No wonder Kashmir is called a disturbed area.", said Ilyas.

I was getting upset now. I had clear information about his indulgence in nefarious activities. "Should I use third degree?," I thought, "But no, the case is already in the limelight and I have clearly violated a few rules of operation."

"You see Saheb! I recently got into an altercation with my neighbour in the village. He had encroached into my area on the fields. One of the sides of my orchard is not fenced. I have reasons to believe it's at his behest that I have been implicated. Mohd Rafiq Khan has a close relative in the territorial Army set up at Handwara.", Ilyas interjected my thought process.

"Ilyas! Sleep peacefully today. Let those people return in the morning and we shall know the truth.", I said realising that perhaps that was the only way out.

"But Saheb! Please do not hurt me. I am willing to cooperate in every way to prove my innocence. My family must really be worried by my disappearance by now. Many have already disappeared in the past and some never returned.", pleaded Ilyas.

"You have my word on that. But if I find you guilty of anything, I will not spare you tomorrow."

With that I left Ilyas alone. He had been tied down to ensure that he could not escape. The guard had been asked to remain alert. The guard was a huge strain on the company resources and the restraining bonds on the captive Ilyas but both had to be in place. Ilyas could not be allowed the freedom to attempt an escape and be shot in the process. Custodial death would have been a problem of much larger proportions. So, the bonds had to stay and the guard alert.

I slept fitfully the entire night checking every now and then for it to be morning. 8 AM was on my mind as the ikhwanis were to return with detailed information on Ilyas. I spent half the night plotting how I would use the details received to extract the truth from Ilyas. Recovery of a cache of arms would be an event of major highlight for me. I slept fitfully and anxiously.

When the following morning came, I was already awake. Having checked that Ilyas was still fine, I settled down for some breakfast. Now the wait began for 8 AM.

8 AM came and went, but the ikhwanis didn't turn up. My repeated attempts to call up the ikhwanis on their mobile phone was met with a 'the cell is switched off' message. The ikhwanis were completely untraceable. I was red faced. I was both angry and feeling stupid. I had to work hard to maintain my composure. This was a major loss of face of course. I called the team and enquired about the name of the second ikhwani. It was Mohd Azam Khan as someone in my team recollected. So, perhaps Ilyas was right. Perhaps Rafiq and Azam were related after all.

I contacted the company commander in Handwara to enquire about the whereabouts of Ishaq and Azam. Apparently, both were on leave for the week.

In the meantime, it was time to speak to the boss again.

"Maqbool! I am sending down a vehicle with the necessary documentation. Please have Ilyas handed over to the local police station in Handwara and subsequently released to his people.", instructed Haider. Haider showed the composure of a seasoned Commanding Officer. He said nothing to me. Nor asked any difficult questions. Perhaps he understood it all. He must have seen many new company commanders mature over time. Perhaps he too would have travelled along a similar learning curve as a company commander. He simply allowed me to figure it out by myself without embarrassing me.

I still did not know how to face Ilyas. With all that threatening and menacing the previous evening, I had nothing left to show. At least and thankfully, I had spared the third degree. This by itself would be a big defeat for Ishaq and Azam for part of their objective was unrealised. Ilyas was not mistreated even though he had spent an anxious night away from home. Ishaq and Azam had hoped that they could trick me into thrashing Ilyas to extract information. Thankfully the thrashing did not happen. Partly, it was Ilyas' luck.

The paperwork that followed and the process of release took major part of the day. His kith and kin were happy to have Ilyas back. Ilyas told everyone that he was not mistreated at all by me. I was surprised that people had the capability to be thankful and truthful even under duress. People were generally thankful for it to be so. I was, however, still angry with the two ikhwani boys. They had had the audacity to manipulate me into doing something terribly wrong.

Finally, having wasted an entire day with the police, the work was done and everyone could go back home happily.

I was now alone in the vehicle driving back to the op base with a small team when it occurred to me. "Is this what Riyaz meant yesterday?"

"Not everything is as it seems."

"Don't trust people blindly."

I was flustered by the swiftness with which Ishaq had misused my trust. And I was now seething with anger even though I could not openly show it. The internal call to get even was pretty compelling and I began to evaluate plans to sort Ishaq out. There clearly was no legal or official means of doing this though. The reality dawned upon me very quickly that if anything that had gone wrong, then the responsibility was clearly mine. After all, all the glory attached with recovering the cache if it really were to happen, would have been mine too. With no legal means of doing it, the only possible path to a release lay in catching Ishaq and giving him a sound beating. With the powers that I enjoyed, it could clearly be termed official action or better still, no one needed to know the beating ever happened.

I spent the next 24 hours scheming on laying a trap for Ishaq. After 24 hours, once the anger had settled down a bit, I began to think again. It soon dawned upon me that no matter what, I personally had learned a very useful lesson in the entire episode. Furthermore, there were bigger issues waiting for my attention. Nabbing Ishaq would have gotten me nowhere. In the process, I had also been exercised in conducting a swift operation of the kind that I did. I then decided that it was best to ignore the entire episode but to keep the lessons learnt and focus on my primary objective. Ishaq would get sorted out very soon. His objective of pressurising Ilyas had also clearly not worked. If at all, Ilyas now had my support including that of the company commander in his own area.

5

Learning to trust my instincts!

I had learnt a very valuable lesson finally "keep your eyes and ears open, but act only when you are really convinced". One single episode has the power to transform one's personality tremendously. And it couldn't be more true than in my case. I was now suddenly even more open to everything that was being said to me. To create incentives for more and more people to come and speak to me, I became ever so helpful. The word spread and the locals began to come in to fill me with their stories. I knew most just wanted some freebees but I was also sure that in the middle of it, some will still present the real picture. The channels were now open.

"Sir! I had woken up last night to relieve myself and saw 4 dark figures emerging from the neighbour's house.", said one. He had earned for himself and perhaps his poor family a bag of 5 kg of rice.

"Sir! Soon after dark, I often see shadows visit the house of one Mohd Anwar Khan in my village.", this one wanted some milk powder. He had small kids to feed.

"Sir! You must have seen that little forest behind village Sodal. Two terrorists have been operating out of it for last more than a month now.", this guy was given some wheat flour.

And so the information kept flowing. One thing was clear that most such information came from either the weaker sections of the society or from those who wanted to gain proximity to me. And the only way for me to figure out what was authentic and what wasn't, was to cross check. When more than one person pointed at the same piece of information, it's probability of being true increased. Besides, I had to figure out what to do with the information that appeared to be authentic.

The day time and night time patrolling accordingly began to be planned. On having made up my mind on certain pieces of information coming in, I now began to channelise my teams to patrol areas to create a stir as also upset free movement except at times that I wanted.

I wanted to separate the movement of terrorists from that of the civil population. Hence, military presence along likely routes was the key. By the day, presence of a road opening team all along the road that bisected my area into East and West zone automatically prevented free movement of terrorists. It's the segregation at dusk and a little later that was important. Hence, the patrolling teams were moved out at last light to areas around the target area to

conduct what appeared to be routine area domination/
curfew enforcement patrols. Invariably, I accompanied such
patrols. The timings of these patrols were staggered to keep
the people guessing. Astonishingly, as long as the patrols
were out, the area would remain very quiet.

Away from the urban centres, the area remained
pretty quiet at night. Very often though, soon after the
patrols would return, the dogs in the villages would come
alive. It was possible to figure out the general direction and
pin point the village, the sound of the barking dogs came
from. Since villages in the area were in a line, it only helped
further. Thankfully, the dogs had no sympathy for anyone
who was an outsider to the village - Army and terrorists
alike.

I then decided to build a log of the dogs barking. One
of the sentry posts was given the task to do so. The logs
began to tell a story and a clearer picture began to emerge.
Since dogs lived within the villages only, they barked only
when someone approached the fringes or entered the
village. The time interval between successive sets of dogs
barking told a clear story of the direction of the movement.
In most cases, the time interval between the barking dogs in
two separate villages coincided with the time normal
human movement would take between these villages.

The most stunning discovery however, was that most
of the barking or rather nearly all of the barking happened
only after the patrols returned to the op base. Someone was
clearly keeping an eye on the op base and relayed
information whenever a patrol came in or went out of the

base. With mobile phone communication coming in, it was very difficult to figure out who relayed the information. But it was now crystal clear to me that the base was under constant surveillance which was not a very difficult task given that the moment one stepped out of the base, one would encounter villages all around. In fact, there was a village right outside the company's main gate across the road.

With the problem clearly defined, I now had to find ways to solve it. With the dogs' activity logs and the information coming in from the locals, a clear picture of terrorist activities began to emerge. Two terrorists- both locals were operating in and around village Sodal. Sodal was a small village and farthest away from the op base in my territory and lay on the boundary with the neighbouring company's area. It further lay on the fringes of a high ground that was forested on the slopes with the top devoid of any vegetation thus affording good visibility. Anyone sitting on the slopes a little distance above the village could achieve a dominating view of the areas around. A local help placed further above on the table top could provide early warning against any approaching military movement from the high ground above. I, thus, decided to test the hypothesis.

It was a bright sunny day in May- with the Ishaq episode truly behind me, I led a patrol into the area. I purposely decided to avoid the village and take a circuitous route from behind the village to the high ground. I wanted to avoid being picked up by the terrorists directly. My only means of finding out lay in activating the early warning elements if at all they existed. As soon as the patrol reached the high ground, the scouts leading the patrol could spot one person with a few sheep in the area. It wasn't the best pasture for the animals to graze on. As soon as the scouts approached the person, he began to shout pleading to be spared. This was rather odd behaviour because no one had even addressed him. The shouting and crying was clearly a signal for someone else. His position closer to the slopes towards village Sodal and the odd behaviour confirmed my hypothesis. The shepherd's location also pointed at the militants probable location by day.

I pretended not to have found anything odd about the shepherd's shouting. I was sure that a two member team of militants would not want to indulge in a fire fight with my well trained team of twelve. I asked for the shepherd to be hauled upto me. My team too had no idea of what was going on in my mind or what I suspected.

"You sound pretty melodious.", I said to the shepherd. By now the shepherd was quiet having conveyed the message already. If anything, he was not a good actor. His sheepish smile and mannerism gave away the ploy. However, I was a good actor too and pretended not to notice anything amiss.

"What is your name? Where are you from?", I asked.

"Saheb! I am from Sodal and my name is Mohd Arif Khan.", he said. "I had become scared on seeing the Army." The lookout man was ready with an explanation.

"Okay! So why don't you shout some more? You do sound melodious.", I said. An average Kashmiri is pretty soft spoken and not the least loud. So, most men when they shout find it a huge strain on their vocal cords. On shouting, they sound as if they are singing as the pitch breaks often. Kashmiri women on the contrary can be ferociously loud and do not suffer from any such problems.

"I don't want to see you behave like this ever again Arif!", I continued. "The Army is here to look after you all. Don't be scared of the Army."

With that I continued with my patrolling and returned to the op base without once looking towards the village Sodal. My suspicions were mostly confirmed. I was now beginning to firm up my plans and also looking for an opportune moment to strike. A gap of a few days had to be given to make it appear that everything was normal. No one in the base knew anything about the presence of the militants in the area. The dog barking logs and the help seeking informers continued to give a clear picture of the movement in the area. I next decided to completely clear the area of Army patrolling for a week. This was done to put the militants as also their supporters off guard. It was time to prepare.

On the 5th day, the weather suddenly packed up and it began to rain in the evening. Even in the month of May, it had become a little chilly suddenly. The cloud cover gave a clear indication that it was going to remain cloudy, packed and wet and cold for more than 24 hours at least. With the evening games not happening because of the wet conditions, I got thinking.

"Is it an indication from above?"

"Is it the right time to strike."

"Given the inclement weather, the terrorists must tuck in nicely into some supporter's house for the night."

I decided to take the hints from above and my chances. Because of the sudden change in the weather, all operations had been wound up earlier than usual. Even the road opening team was in early. I immediately convened my 'O' group consisting of the team leaders, the Sr. JCO and the CHM. I gave out my orders, the teams were asked to prepare to move out past midnight for a Cordon and search operation. All the teams were already well rehearsed to undertake the operation. Since the village to be searched was in my own area, everyone knew the area and the village well.

I suddenly remembered that since my op base was under surveillance, the surveillance elements would all the more be careful around the usual time that the Army moves out for a cordon which was usually within a couple of hours past midnight. I next decided to delay the departure time to 5 AM - a time that most Kashmiris are busy with morning ablutions or in case of a cold wet morning, perhaps cozying up in bed still. I anticipated by then even the surveillance elements would have given up on any early morning movement out of our base.

This time I chose to inform Haider well in advance about my plans. Haider in turn promised to keep back up and reinforcements ready in case of any eventuality. Additionally, he had to be informed that no troops were available for the road opening in the morning. This was vital information for everyone.

At 4.30 AM, the teams had assembled behind the barracks away from where they could be seen from outside the op base. The briefing now commenced. Everyone had collected their morning breakfast, some had even consumed it. The cookhouse had been activated 2 hours earlier. It took as much time to get breakfast ready and packed for the company by 4 AM. It had rained the entire night and it was cold. When the teams assembled, the rain had slowed down to a drizzle.

"Bad weather is God's gift to a soldier." I remembered having been told so during our training at the academies. It seemed to be coming true now.

The boys were looking upbeat and raring to go after a good night's sleep. I had hardly slept. Firstly, I was used to sleeping not before 2 AM on other days for I believed that someone out of the senior leadership in the company should be awake at all times. Late nights, I had chosen for myself. Besides, the adrenaline of what was to come had me strangely excited. And a sub conscious anticipation of a gun fight that day had kept me further alert. The getting out of bed is the strangest in such a situation. I hadn't slept the entire night and now closer to waking up time, I wanted to grab the very last minutes of rest possible in bed. For coming up was a marathon session with not an iota of an opportunity to rest in the middle. In fact, to the contrary, I had to have the sharpest of my wits around. Each one of these is a test that I could not hope to fail. For me, failure simply meant a loss of life within my team. In case of a loss, I felt getting any number of terrorists or weapons would become inconsequential.

I had a major role to play. With more than 70 of my team members in deployment with weapons, there was a massive fire power in use. I had to continuously be mindful of every single team members' location, monitoring who is doing what, while being in the middle of the most crucial part - the house to house search, ensuring there is no cross fire between own troops. Hence, I needed to be completely focused onto the task at hand and nothing else. Distractions of any kind could be lethal.

The team was now ready for briefing. I was completely ready myself. I was wearing my combat dress with my most comfortable shoes with layers of socks - nylons on the inside and a woollen one outside. This prevented foot sores or blisters of any kind. I was going to be on my feet the whole day. A bullet proof jacket was the outermost layer. Inside I wore the coat parka which was water proof and protected against the cold as well. I carried a 9mm Browning pistol as a side arm with 14 bullets loaded. A sort of insurance in case my main weapon - the 7.62mm AK-47 rifle jammed up on me. Besides, I carried a well sharpened khukri which every Gurkha soldier carried with him in combat. The khukri was a versatile weapon especially in hand to hand combat and most importantly, it was part of the Gurkha tradition. I had a radio set slung in the upper part of my jacket attached to a headset which I would use whenever I needed to be handsfree for communication. Wearing a cap as of then, I had my bullet proof patka ready to be worn when going in for the search or whenever the risk was high - this choice was my privilege. Everyone else had to wear the patka at all times. The men were identically dressed less the pistol and carried a small back pack additionally with a water bottle and packed food. Only the team leaders carried radio sets. Below that in hierarchy, communication was going to be verbal and based on hand signals.

I quickly carried out an inspection of the team ensuring the boys were well kitted and looking healthy and visibly upbeat inspite of the gloomy weather. A soldier has an inbuilt sixth sense that allows him to sense when something's going to happen. Accordingly, everyone appeared to be in a serious mood. This was very different from the routine.

"There is information of 2 terrorists in village Sodal. In all likelihood, they are inside the village as of now. Our company will conduct a cordon and search operation of village Sodal and neutralise the two militants. Teams 1, 2, 3 and 4 will establish cordon around the village from the South, East, West and North, respectively. Team 5 will be in reserve on the high ground above the village. My QRT[11] will enter the village and be present near the community

---

[11] Quick Reaction Team - the Company Commander's best trained team was called so. Its strength lay in the ability to move faster than other teams.

centre and subsequently conduct a search of the village. On congregating the villagers, team 5 will provide protection to the villagers and carry out a census basis the village census register. Throughout the operation, everyone will be in buddy pairs and remain under cover. No one will open fire unless you see a target clearly and as close as 100 metres or less to you. Be also mindful of things happening around you. If you notice anything out of place, report in. Be in touch with the one to your left and to your right. All the best! Any questions?" The briefing went smoothly.

Since there were no questions, I continued, "We have two civil vehicles waiting outside. We need to quickly mount, reach the location and establish the cordon before anyone realises. Team nos. 1, 2, 3, 4 will move on priority."

I had already tasked the main gate guard to impound two civil vehicles for the job even before I moved out for the briefing. For the purpose, a milk van and a dumper truck had been stopped - their purpose altered for the time being. The teams moved with swiftness such that in next 40 minutes the cordon had been established in a village 6 kms away. By the time my QRT and team 5 had fetched up to the village, the report of the teams in place had come in over radio from the respective team leaders and it was still dark. People had perhaps not anticipated this before. Most cordons were generally laid around 2 or 3 AM and this one was much later. People were in for a surprise. The simultaneous laying of the cordon had not allowed for anyone to make a getaway. The villagers having realised that the Army had moved in, knew what was to come next. They were far more experienced than me in the matter.

I spent the next 2 hours simply observing the village. The villagers had their morning routines to take care of. A quick bite before perhaps getting to spend a day out of homes. The villagers referred to this form of Army operation as a 'crackdown'. These many years into the situation, the local population was quite used to it. For me, however, this was one of the first few. I had had some training though but a real event is a real event.

'Cordon and search operation' is much like a game of hide and seek. Bad elements get sufficient time to hide and prepare before the Army moves in. As of now, the Army was located on the fringes only and not inside the village. It is a rather dangerous operation. The place of hiding and situating themselves for a contest with the security forces is left to the terrorists. Hence, they get all the time to plan a mini battle of sorts.Till such time that they are either detected in their hideout or they open fire, the initiative is with the terrorists. The first salvo fired by them can be extremely dangerous. Hence, it was important that from the moment they opened fire first and contact established, they are not allowed to break contact. Breaking contact would give them the opportunity to fire the second 'first salvo'.

Having waited long enough for the local people to have sorted their preparedness for the day long event, I decided it was time to roll out the next phase. Until then, no one from the village was allowed to leave or anyone allowed to go into the village.

The first visible person was asked to go into the village mosque that was equipped with an announcement system and announce the 'crackdown' asking all the villagers to assemble at the village community centre. It appeared as if the villagers were waiting for the announcement for within the next fifteen minutes, everyone was out of their houses and congregated at the community centre. Once the village population had congregated, I called for the megaphone and addressed the gathered public.

"I am sorry that you have been inconvenienced in the morning like this. We suspect a few terrorists are hiding in the village and we are here to flush them out. It will be our endeavour to make it happen with minimum loss of life or property. We expect you to cooperate with us in the matter. In case anyone here faces any problems, please feel free to let us know. Before we enter the village, I need to know if anyone has anything to report?", I announced to the villagers.

No one said anything. I then decided to proceed with the search operation along with my QRT. The villagers had, during the announcement from the mosque, been instructed to leave their houses open for the search.

I had decided to have minimum force inside the village. In my own team of 12, I decided to keep six in the search with the remaining six in reserve dominating the house where search was taking place while simultaneously cutting off the side of the village where I did not want the terrorists to run towards, in case of a fire exchange.

I had picked up four young men from amongst the villagers to accompany the search team as witnesses while also helping with opening and closing of houses for search. Their credentials had been established before the search began. A soldier is expected to keep his hands on his weapon ready to fire if needed at all times. Taking hands off the weapon and lifting and shifting things on one's own can be hazardous. Hence, the local villagers were chosen for the job.

The drill was simple. The local boys go in first as no one in the village had owned up to the presence of any terrorists in the village. They open the windows and close the doors of each room in the house being searched. On coming out, they report if the house is clear of any human presence. If they reported that the house was clear, they accompanied the soldiers back into the house. The Army per force had to enter from the front door. I had decided that only 4 of the team would enter- the two scouts, me and my buddy with the four village boys. The team quickly flushes out the rooms to ensure no human presence while closing the doors behind them to reach the top of the house. Once on the top, search would be undertaken starting from top to bottom. This is when detailed search including for specially constructed hideouts is carried out. The remaining two soldiers remained outside the house being searched ready to react to any situation that may develop.

The house to house search operation is perilous for both the seeker and those hiding. However, those hiding have the advantage of choosing the scene of combat and thus of opening fire first. The first burst fired by the terrorists is the riskiest and most dangerous and where soldiers' lives could be lost. Once the contact is established, the seeker has the advantage in terms of numerical superiority. However, those hiding can be smart and chose to multiply the seeking by firing once, running to a new place and then firing again. My job was to ensure to cut the seeking to just once and if possible judge even that 'once' before it happened. An animal strikes only when the animal is cornered and feels endangered. The idea was to corner the militant and allow them the luxury of thinking that they were not, making them think that they had a way out. Additionally, I was relying on the body language of the villagers that I thought could give the situation out.

Thus, began the search. The first house was successfully cleared. I placed the reserve half of the team deeper into the village to cut off any militant running out of the houses being searched. I deliberately began to slow down the search operation. It was subconsciously a game of nerves. Who could psyche up the other side faster? I could sense that if the terrorists are hiding in the village, it must be made terrible for them to wait cramped up, in some corner away from light, and perhaps making it difficult for them to breathe. The longer they remained in that position, the more reckless they could become.

By the time, the search had proceeded and cleared the first eight houses of a total of twenty six, nothing much had happened. Two hours had gone by and the search was getting tiring. I was continuously ordering and controlling everyone's movement. We had come pretty deep into the village. Next up was a double storied house made mostly of wood with an external wooden staircase leading up to the I floor from the left side of the house, which was rather odd and unlike houses in Kashmir.

I ordered the village boys to enter the house and open all the windows while leaving the doors closed. This was done so that one could look inside without allowing anyone inside the house to move between rooms undetected.

The villagers entered the rooms on the ground floor and very soon stepped out having complied. However, the access to the upper floor was not from the inside. They then proceeded to the first floor using the external staircase very quickly opening the windows on the first floor and coming out. But as they proceeded to come down from the stairs, they stopped on the top of the staircase and looked at each other. Even though they exchanged glances for a fraction of a second, I could pick it up and sensed something was amiss. Next as a matter of routine, I summoned the villagers to me and asked if they had seen someone or something in the house. "Nahi Janab!", came the reply. I quickly grabbed one of them by the arm and led him up the stairs. My team followed my lead.

The team stormed into the rooms on the I floor. But those were empty. I was perplexed. I was sure I would find something there. A detailed search followed. But nothing, nothing was found. I was even more confused. I was sure from the momentarily observed body language of the boys that something was not right. I was now standing on top of the staircase with my buddy wondering why the villagers had behaved as they had. Looking around and observing things in the house, I ordered the rest of them to move down and commence search of the lower floor. As everyone moved down, I looked around one last time. Half hopeful I would find the reason for the villagers behaviour and half in despair that I might have missed what happened there or worse still, there was nothing really.

As I turned to move down the stairs and rejoin the search party below, I finally spotted it. Next to the staircase was the animal shed and on top of it, hiding amidst a heap of firewood was a human being as one of his ears became clearly visible from where I stood. Standing on the ground, it would have been impossible to see the person. Perhaps hiding there for long would have made him fidgety, making the firewood to come loose and exposing his ear. Even then at a distance of less than 10 metres, I was not sure if I could open fire for it was still not confirmed whether these were indeed terrorists in the first place and if they were, were they willing to surrender or contest. Such are the exigencies of service that with no other logic for someone hiding the way this man was, I still had to wait for him to perhaps fire first. Hence, my immediate reaction was to shout and get myself and my team under cover and into safety. I and my buddy literally jumped off the staircase to take cover below.

The dilemma in my mind was soon broken as the terrorists - two of them, sensing they had been detected opened fire from where they hid. Luckily, for me and my team, we were well below the terrorist's line of fire and hence safe as the bullets flew overhead. The terrorists now rose out of their cover and were immediately engaged by my team. One of the terrorists fell on the spot dead while the other jumped from the top of the shed while still firing simultaneously. The immediate reaction of my team was to duck for cover. The terrorist now ran behind the house trying to get deeper into the village. Thankfully for my team, the other half was well located to handle the situation. The reserve half opened fire in one short crisp burst and in less than ten seconds, the engagement was over.

Everything was now deafeningly silent. All the chatter had died down. The radios were silent - nothing could be heard not even footsteps. The world had apparently frozen for that moment. It took what felt like a long time for things to restart. The first thing I heard was my own breathing and I could sense my chest swelling and emptying with my breathing - I was breathing hard. Next, I began to hear my heart beat, sounding like loud thuds in between my ears. It took a few more seconds for me to gather my wits. I looked at my buddy who was crouching besides me. I realised he had been shielding me from any fire that might come towards us.

"Are you alright?", I asked my buddy.

"Ji Saheb!", replied Sarabjit.

It was still very quiet when the radio opened up.

"Haider for Maqbool", came the voice. The boss having heard the exchange of fire and its subsequent stoppage wanted to know what had happened. Unknown to me, the boss with his QRT had fetched up to the village almost an hour earlier and was interacting with the villagers not wanting to disturb me.

"Maqbool for Haider! Over!", I replied as per radio protocol.

"What is the situation?", asked Haider.

"I will come back. Wait!", I messaged.

I now asked my reserve half team leader, "Maqbool for Phale!". Phale was the half team leader's name - a hardened Gurkha NCO[12], handpicked by me a few months earlier for my team. Of course, his real name was a lot longer, Phale was the short form of it.

"Phale for Maqbool - Euta terrorist payo hajoor!", said Phale confirming having shot down one terrorist in the Nepalese language over radio. Haider would have heard that too.

"Phale! Is everyone alright?", I enquired.

"Hajoor", came the crisp reply.

I then called out to my half of the team to find if everything was alright. To my relief, no one was even injured. The villagers accompanying the team were absent from the scene. When I shouted for them, they came out from one of the rooms on the ground floor where they had huddled together. They knew exactly when the fire fight was going to break out and further knew where to getaway in the shortest possible time for their own safety.

---

[12] Non-commissioned Officer

Now came the difficult task of ascertaining whether the terrorists were really dead and there were no more of them in hiding. I ordered a few shots be fired towards the cowshed top hoping to draw fire if anyone was still alive. As no fire came back, I with my buddy climbed the staircase to get a closer view of the cowshed top for a second time. This time I could clearly see a terrorist lying dead on top. As I went further up, I could see the second terrorist lying dead on the pathway behind the house. Surprisingly, the house had access from this side as well as the one in front which was again unlike most Kashmiri houses which have single access only. I could also establish an eye contact with the other half of my team and nodded in approval. The Gurkha soldiers smiled back appearing completely relaxed and in control of themselves. I was not half as relaxed. I now decided to give the report to my boss.

"Maqbool for Haider!", I called on the radio. Perhaps the entire battalion that could listen in being on the same frequency, was waiting to hear this.

"Haider for Maqbool! Go on!"

"Sir! We have got two. Identity not known. Yet to make recoveries of weapons and ammunition. Team is fine. No one is hurt. No loss of property either.", I reported.

"Good! Whose house did you find them in?", "Is it Mir Chopan's house?", Haider asked before I could reply to the first question.

I turned to the villagers to ask the name of the house owner. It was indeed Mir Chopan's house.

"Yes sir!", I replied, completely perplexed.

"How did Haider know?", I thought to himself. "I would ask him later."

In less than 5 minutes, Haider had fetched up to where I was with his team. His team quickly spread out. The team NCO closely observing 'the kills'.

"Good afternoon sir!", I said. "I am absolutely intrigued to know how did you know it was Mir Chopan's house?"

"You see there was one lady in the congregation who was crying uncontrollably. She belongs to this house. The locals always know if something is wrong and she must have feared that her house could get completely destroyed in the gun battle.", said Haider.

I realised I too had seen a lady crying earlier in the day in the congregation but it never occurred to me that this could be the reason.

"Leave it to my team to handle the mopping up activities and moving the dead bodies further to the battalion headquarters and for onward disposal. They have been specially trained for this. You may observe though.", said Haider. "You can de-induct your teams after that and break the congregation of the villagers.", instructed Haider.

Haider was personally going to oversee the retrieval of the dead bodies. Of course, the villagers came in handy. A tractor with a trolley was arranged on which the dead bodies were loaded and taken to the battalion headquarters.

I did not know but Haider did. Terrorists in the past had booby trapped their own bodies just before dying using hand grenades by removing the pin and trapping the grenade under their bodies such that when the dead body is moved, the hammer of the grenade would be let loose to set off the grenade resulting in casualties. Haider had trained his team to ensure that no such accidents would take place. It was an education for me. Of course, Haider's learning had come from an accident in the past. I was lucky to have him around.

Once the entire operation was over within the village, an NOC[13] was obtained from the village elders. The cordon was lifted and the teams de-inducted to the op base. Since everyone in the area knew about the ongoing operation, the de-inducting forces could sometimes become an easy prey for booby traps, IEDs[14] and even ambushes. Hence, the de-induction needed to be well planned. Troops, tired out after a full day in operations were in a hurry to get back. Hence, the movement of teams was well staggered and conducted using different routes. I and my QRT were the last to leave the village. The villagers had been let into the village well before that. I chose to not say anything to the villagers which by itself was a surprise for the villagers since some militants had been found in the village. It was a departure from the practice in the past for the villagers, where some other Company Commander would have spent time lecturing them on their wrong doings. For me, it was not the case. I was calm, jubilant even since the operation had

---

[13] No objection certificate

[14] Improvised Explosive Devices

gone well - no one in my team was hurt and we had successfully got two terrorists.

By the time, I arrived back at the base, everyone was in a joyous mood. The operation was a success. Neighbouring company commanders had called in to congratulate me. Very soon, even the sector commander - Haider's boss, called to congratulate me on the success. The operation had closed in good time and all were settled back by 5 PM. I knew the teams had been baptised by fire and I could now call myself experienced. The company's confidence had soared significantly. The troops were visibly happy having seen the leadership with which I had conducted the operation.

I had been invited for the customary picture with 'the kills' at the battalion headquarters. I refused. Somewhere deep down, I did not enjoy the sight of the dead bodies. I was done with them though I wanted to know their identities. The battalion was generally happy with the operation. It was a good start to the 'campaigning season'[15]. I had also decided against a customary 'barakhana'[16] to celebrate 'the kills'. For me, someone's death - even that of terrorists was not to be a reason for celebrations. I did choose to complement the men in the operation and the company in general for the success. But I could also sense what was to come - things had only just started.

---

[15] A term used for the summer months when the number of terrorist activities increase in the valley.

[16] A celebratory lavish dinner organised in which all officers and other ranks dine together.

The first thing to hit was the thought that kept me awake that night.

"What if the terrorist's bullets had hit?"

To divert the thought, I watched one movie after another late into the night until I slept exhausted. By the next morning, the thoughts had gone. I decided that I needed to keep myself and the men busy to avoid such a stress building up. It was only later I was to learn that this is called 'post traumatic stress' - something that plays heavily with the minds of people who have been into stressful situations that endanger lives. However, the solution to the problem was correctly found by me, even before I knew what I was doing.

6

A close miss!

The word of the operation spread. Not only the Army personal but also the civil population was talking about it. By now, I knew who the militants were. Local messages on the radio to their handlers across the border had been intercepted where the incident had been reported. Both the terrorists belonged to the Hizbul Mujahideen (HM). Though not from the area originally, they had chosen to operate here since one of them had an aunt in the village. Visits to the aunt had lead to an interest in one of the local girls. The frequent visits to the aunt because of the love interest got them killed. The stories begin to unravel once the information becomes inconsequential.

The elimination of the two terrorists operating in the area had lifted a major pressure off the local population. Threats of extortion on business people reduced significantly. The general pressures felt by the public due to enforcement of the militants' ideology also reduced. The

people were suddenly beginning to feel a little free. The
'Over Ground Workers' (OGWs) backed by these militants
also lost significance to an extent.

I, of course was most intrigued by the fact that the
militant identities were revealed by the interception of
radio communication between the terrorists and their
handlers across the LOC. I, thus, decided to go across to the
Battalion Headquarters to meet this team of interceptors
and see how they operated.

The following day, I travelled across to the Bn HQ
which was located at Magam - a good 15 Kms from the
company op base. The radio surveillance cell was part of
the team of Signalmen at the Battalion Headquarters. Aslam
was the man on duty. He could understand all local
languages besides Hindi and English. He hailed from
Kashmir itself and loved his job. He had spent more than a
thousand hours listening in on the radio networks and
clearly understood the militant groups and their call signs.

The Lashkar-e-Taiba or LeT in North Kashmir had a G
series to designate their top operating terrorists in the
region. Only the top ten had radio sets and call signs from
G1 to G10. When one of these died or was eliminated,
another took his place. Presently, G3 was heading the
organisation. The hallmark of the LeT network in Kashmir
was the mix of Pakistani Punjabi and Urdu language they
used to communicate in. On the radio network, they were
very well behaved. Very few HM militants had radio sets.
Rarely anyone from the other tanzeems surfaced on the
radio net.

The controller across the LoC could be heard clearly, while sitting in Magam. They had strong transmitters. Sometimes, one could only hear the controllers from across and not the stations this side. Today was one such moment where the control in Kotli was talking to a station in Rafiabad and taking stock of an encounter there. Three terrorists had been shot in the area.

"So, which are the active radio stations in our area?", I asked.

"Sir! G3, G5, G6, G7, G8 and G9 operate on the fringes of your company territory bordering with 21 RR to the South. I believe from the strength of their signals, they operate more in the 21 RR area but sometimes do come close. Besides them, of course the two that you neutralised recently could be heard but their station has gone dead now.", replied Aslam with the eagerness of a young man who loved his job.

"Interestingly, one day last year Haider learnt about one of our patrols that was lethargic through the militant radio network. This was before you came. That team got a real mouthful from Haider on radio itself. The whole battalion could hear that.", continued Aslam almost chuckling with laughter. "We are unable to catch any local transmissions north of Magam because of this high hill feature. So we have another surveillance post in one of our company locations to that side."

"So, that is quite boring and very little chatter to deal with.", I remarked.

"No sir! Once in a while I talk to these terrorists operating in our area using their call signs especially when I can make out one of their call signs has been idle for a while. I can do it quite convincingly. They talk in the plain but use codewords for locations and people here in their conversation. I spend a lot of time trying to figure out what these codewords for places really mean on ground. And then with Haider's help, we are able to move our patrols such that we can trap some of these terrorists. We were successful in getting two such terrorists to move to an area we figured out successfully. Haider then had an ambush set up and luckily we had an encounter where we got one kill.", said Aslam proudly. "Of course! I only knew we had correctly decoded the place after the encounter took place. They have never used the same codeword again ever after."

"You see sir! It is a very interesting job and I have been contributing in my own way.", said Aslam.

"I see! It must require a lot of intelligence and diligence to make it happen Aslam."

"So which are the other regular call signs nearby?", I asked. "How did we identify the two terrorists in Sodal?"

"Oh that was easy. It was thanks to Beg. Beg is a reporter for the terrorists in our area. From the strength of his radio transmissions, I suspect he lives in Magam or close by. Haider knows it too but we have not been able to identify this man. If anything happens in our area, it is his job to find out what has happened and report the matter. On the night after the operation took place, Beg reported elimination of Hamza and Nabi with all the details as we know them. Hamza was having an affair with Mir Chopan's niece in the same village. Beg is also required to conduct an enquiry to figure out how you knew about the two terrorists. So far, he has not been able to find out or report.", said Aslam. "Of course only you know who informed you about their presence in the village."

I kept quiet. I was not going to share my secret with anyone. It was difficult for many to believe that casual talking, dog barking logs and a dash of plain luck had done it for me.

"These tanzeems like to avenge the elimination of the terrorists by eliminating the informer. I believe so far they have not been able to pin point the informer.", said Aslam.

I thanked Aslam for helping me out. I also made a note of the frequencies Aslam listened in on especially that of Beg and the G series. It was going to be my signal NCO's (back at the op base) new favourite pass time.

On getting back to my op base, I summoned my own signalman - an experienced hand with more than 15 years of service. I handed over the frequencies of the militant organisations to the Signal NCO and asked him to see if he could get a fix on the G series and Beg. Knowing both those operated close to my op base had me intrigued. The signalman was now going to log calls by Beg as also the G series and others he could listen in on. I was excited. Success can do that to a man.

In the meantime, I had become more and more popular - I was approachable, listened to people's problems and solved what I could and sympathised with what I couldn't and most importantly ridiculed those that appeared baseless. Additionally, I was just and believed in treating people fair and giving them the benefit of doubt whenever encountered while treating people with equanimity. To top it all, a successful and well conducted operation in Sodal had added to this popularity. I was a complete package in the eyes of all. People were most impressed by the fact that no one had the slightest inkling as to who the informer was. For all those who wanted to help the Army, this was a big plus in my favour. Resultantly, more and more people started to come forth and talk to me. Of course, only I knew the truth.

Information was beginning to flow in at an alarming rate but most of it was not actionable. The summers had come in and the days had become quite long. Activity in the farms and apple orchards had increased manifold. Since the nights had become really short, operating in stealth had become difficult.

I was keeping an eye on the radio logs now. The G series was surfacing at regular intervals. G3 and G9 radio transmissions were particularly clear and strong and the closest of the lot. Yet no information of theirs came through the villagers I met. I concluded that they had to be operating out of the neighbouring areas.

I was also now beginning to meet prominent people in my own area. Some of them came multiple times and became good friends. Akbar was one such person. He was the son of the Sarpanch of the largest village in the area. The last Panchayat elections happened a long time back. The

Sarpanch had officially outlived the duration in office. But since elections had not happened in a long time, people continued to refer to him as Sarpanch. He looked to be a pious and calm old man with eyes that told a lot of sad stories. Yet he was someone who maintained his composure in all situations. He was much respected by the local population. His son - Akbar on the contrary was extremely jovial and social. He loved to spend time out of home and was well connected to a few politicians in Srinagar who were also his friends. Akbar was in mid 30s and married with kids.

I do not remember how Akbar and I met for the first time but we both hit it off instantly. Akbar had a knack of striking the right chords and saying just the right things. He particularly liked to talk about the history of his village and the surrounding areas which was of keen interest to me. No one ever breached the more sensitive or sad topics such as the exodus of Kashmiri pandits from the valley. We both loved to talk. To spice up the chats, I would sponsor the beer while Akbar brought in home cooked delicious wazwan[17]. I was now beginning to appreciate Kashmiri cuisine - the Rista being my favourite already. Sundays now became interesting and enjoyable. For me, it was a good break from the high stress routine and also a good dose of local history. In the process, I also learnt a lot about the people to people equations in the village Akbar came from. I always suspected that some villagers had to be complicit

---

[17] A name for the traditional Kashmiri cuisine.

with militant activities but somehow there was a complete information blackout in Shehlal - the village Akbar came from. No one ever talked about any militant activity which was a big surprise.

In the meantime, Beg continuously reported about the happenings in the area which the Signal NCO intercepted. The reports were few but invariably the enquiries from across centred around the Sodal episode. They were unable to pin point the information source and sounded desperate.

The pressure created by the successful operation in the area had to be sustained and I was not going to let the momentum dampen. Thus, I kept up with continuous follow up patrols and operations in the area. On one such routine patrol through the villages, I was headed towards Sodal a good thirty days after the encounter in Sodal. I made it a point to meet as many people as possible on the way. On reaching Sodal, I spoke to the people to understand if everything was normal. I, by now, was familiar with the faces of the villagers and conversely, the villagers were familiar with me. Sodal also happened to be half way to Magam on the internal road. Remarkably, the people had completely forgotten or chose to ignore as no one seemed to even hint at the episode that had occurred the previous month. People even appeared normal. I wondered what made them so stoic. While the thought was still transcending through my mind, I happened to notice someone I became instantly curious about. He was moving around aimlessly or so it appeared to me. I asked for the person to be summoned upto me.

"Islam e wallekum!", said the man.

"Wallekum Islam! Who are you? I haven't seen you here before.", I asked already a little taken aback by the man's confidence.

"Sir! I am from Magam. I am Mohd Ayaz Khan. I have come here to visit my sister who lives in Sodal.", said Aslam.

"OK! What do you do Ayaz?"

"Sir! I am unemployed. I surrendered in 1999 and ever since do small jobs here and there.", said Aslam.

"OK! That is good to know. Why don't you come and meet me sometime. You can let me know whenever you are coming. My number is advertised in the area.", I said closing with words which were almost standard remark by me in such conversations now. I and my team moved on and returned to base in due course of time. I was largely convinced that no terrorist was stationed in the area for long or operating out of it. I had come to learn from Haider how to judge the situation through people's body language. Of course, some transit of militants through the area could not be ruled out.

The radio logs, however, clearly pointed towards a significant chatter between the G series and their control across. Beg appeared to be under pressure but the Sodal case was now closed in the absence of any headway in the area. The larger battalion area comprising of six smaller company areas like the one I was responsible for, appeared to be largely quiet. No untoward episodes had been reported in the near past.

I was confident that information from my area on movement of bad elements or lack of it was satisfactorily reaching me. But this was largely true for the area north of my op base. Two villages to my South were inadequately covered and their close proximity to the town Handwara made it difficult for me to interact with people of these villages. An occasional trip to the villages or setting up a checkpost on the bridge which was the entry point into the area from Handwara were the only means of interacting with people from these villages. The rest of the area was adequately covered. However, a third part was the forested area in my territory. The same forest that provided access to village Bakiakar on the other side and known by the same name. Of course, no one resided in the forest and village Bakiakar was under the area of responsibility of the neighbouring battalion while the forest was mine.

The forest itself was beautiful. A beautiful stream with clear waters ran along the datum level in the forest that had its origins as well in a spring within the forest itself. The crystal clear water of the stream was lined with beautiful soft fluffy grass growing naturally along the stream banks devoid of any shrubs or weeds for upto 50 meters on either side. The forest was extremely picturesque and a great picnic spot in the past. Unfortunately, with the militants brewing trouble, only the likes of terrorists in the past and now my team could enjoy the beauty of the place. I often routed my own patrols through the forest. It afforded me close proximity to nature and the element of surprise since the team in the forest could rarely be under surveillance. Besides, the forest needed to be kept sanitised.

To overcome the problem of the surveillance on the camp, I had an alternate 'chor rasta' made to provide movement in and out of the camp quietly. Additionally, to avoid detection, I would sometimes move out in a very small team of just six people. Today was another one of those nights when I had decided to venture into the Bakiakar forest with just a very small team of six. I had selected five of my best to operate alongside after series of iterations in the field. This team of six could literally move like ghosts undetected. I preferred a small team in the forest for the need to have good command and control. A large team on a dark night in the forest can be extremely difficult to manage.

On the fateful day, I with my team of six left the op base in the morning at 3 AM with the objective of observing the forest early in the morning. The team left using the 'chor rasta'. Once out of the post, the team walking along the stream was in the forest in less than 15 minutes. It was one of those dark nights completely devoid of any moonlight. The moon was in the 4th quarter. In the forest, it was so dark that one could not see one's own hand. In such a scenario, the team was moving forward purely dependent on one's instincts, ears and fortune. Every 200 yards, the team would stop and listen intently for any sounds emanating ahead of them. It appeared to be one of those nights when everything was extremely still. Not even the wind was blowing. And thankfully for that, since that could have created illusions difficult to deal with.

The forest seemed deserted - not even animals were encountered on the night. It was usual otherwise to spot a couple of bears, leopards and sometimes even tigers at night through the thermal imagers the lead scout carried. I had long since refused to use the thermal imager after the first time I did. I was unable to adjust to the loss of dilation of the pupils after seeing through the sight once. It takes a long time for the eyes to adjust to the darkness. And I found it extremely difficult. The lead scout 'Tale' however, was an expert - the perfect scout, again discovered through numerous iterations with other alternatives. He could manage the thermal imager with one hand, his weapon with the other, walk like a ghost - never breaking even a twig at night and when it snowed, his feet never went deep into the standing snow. He was nimble footed and fast. By day, he was even better. He could detect movement on mountains miles away. I was in awe of his skills. He even remembered the routes within the company area of responsibility like the back of his hand. If Tale had been there once, he could get there blind folded. I completely trusted him to be the point man on my team blindly.

The team now climbed through a particularly stiff slope on a hill side. It was dark and the floor infested with bushes. As the team climbed and neared the crest on the hillside, I decided to halt the team. It had already been an hour and a half since the team left the op base. I knew it was going to be first light soon and I did not want to be in the open. I directed my team to take cover and lay an ambush until daylight. Just beyond where the team took up the position was another small valley going down about hundred meters with thick vegetation. In the midst of it, lay a pond which was rarely visited. Across the valley lay another table top where I had met Riyaz and at the bottom of the slope beyond was the village Bakiakar.

"What would Riyaz be doing at the moment? I haven't heard from him in a while.", I thought lying on the ground.

Once in position, the team took five minutes to settle down. With the breathing settled, it was again suddenly very quiet. The team now waited for the morning. When morning finally came, it was full of tranquility. Earlier it was just quiet, now it was also visibly still. Again no wind, everything stood still. The villages around had just about woken up, the morning 'azaan' from the mosques had been sounded and it was quiet again. From on top of the ridge - the highest point in the forest, one could look quite far in all directions. Some hearths had been lit up in the village Bakiakar and smoke could be seen escaping from the chimneys in a few houses. But no movement was visible. In the distant sky, a flock of birds could be seen high up in the sky flying north. The sun was not yet out but it was light enough. From the position of the team the entire table top in the forest was visible including the spot where I had met Riyaz a couple of months earlier. There was no movement whatsoever. In the far distance to the west, the snow peaked mountain tops could be seen - that is where the LoC was and all the terrorists came in from.

The trance like state that I was in, was suddenly disturbed by the loud cackling of some birds in the depression where the water pond was. It appeared that someone or something had suddenly disturbed the birds nesting in the area who flew out with a shriek to take evasive action. I at first thought it could be some other animal prowling in the valley floor that was barely 50 meters below the ridge. Visibility of course was severely restricted due to the presence of a thick underbrush and the trees. I decided to explore what disturbed the birds. After all there was nothing else left to do.

I signalled my team to emerge and walk along the ridge line that encircled the area the sound came from. The team walked as cautiously as possible without making any noise whatsoever. The team had barely walked 50 meters forward when some metallic sound could be heard coming from the same area of the pond. It was like the sound produced from the clanking of some small utensils against each other. The sound itself was for a very brief period of time lasting not more than 2-3 seconds. Clearly, it could have only happened due to human presence. I signalled for my team to take cover, lie dogo and listen carefully. It was again very quiet. My head was racing now.

"Did I really hear the metallic sound or was it my imagination?", I thought. "Should we venture in to explore the valley floor?"

"Are we well equipped?"

To answer the first question, I turned to my buddy and then the scouts. Both seemed to confirm having heard the sound. Their eyes clearly revealed so. I was now sure something was wrong down there. I had to now assess the course of action to be taken.

A jungle search is a very tricky operation. In most cases, a hiding terrorist can see the search party coming in and can prepare to engage well in advance. Since the search is conducted top down, the bottom and the top of the slopes need to be covered and sealed with stops. Given the thick underbrush, it was impossible to maintain surprise in search. The one on the move is at a disadvantage. A militant could very easily engage, hurt and get away. With a small team of just six, it was a rather risky operation with no clear advantage in our favour. I had a difficult choice to make. Go for glory and risk losing a few lives or come back with the right sized force to obviate the disadvantage of that day. I chose the later. I was certain that the elements down below could have picked up my team's presence and may be that is why they had become silent. Sound carries far along the downslopes on hills. Another pretension had to be made. I was a good actor.

"It has been useless coming here this morning.", I said to my team directing the scouts to take the well known beaten track back to base. "I don't know why I even come this side." I was hoping the elements down there had heard me and bought the story.

By day, it was a short walk back to the camp. It took all of 25 minutes to cover a distance that had taken nearly 2 hours at night. The morning report to Haider was due and for a change I had something to say more than just the routine.

"Maqbool for Haider! There has been an interesting development in the Bakiakar forest this morning, during our early morning patrolling.", I said on radio.

"Good! Go on!", Haider was crisp with his communication.

"We detected some human presence in area Pond and I am sure it has got to be some bad elements. I was with a very small team and hence chose not to engage. But we must go back and flush them out. I have a fix on the spot.", I said. Area pond was a well known landmark for use within the battalion. Both Haider and I knew the landmark.

"Alright! Let us meet in the area later in the evening. I am going to call the neighbouring company commander as well. We can plan an operation accordingly.", said Haider and hung up.

Working a night shift leaves one groggy and I was soon asleep. By the time, I woke up, it was already past noon. The meeting with Haider was due in about 4 hours. It was decided to meet at a hill top that allowed for a clear view of the area that I had visited in the morning. This was the best that could be done without alarming the elements that operated in the area. My team was already prepared to leave by 2PM as I had decided to take a circuitous route to avoid going through the forest - the best I could do to not disturb the area.

I decided to go from the north through village Shehlal and reached the place decided for the meeting by 3.30 PM. The hill top afforded an excellent view of the area of interest. Shortly thereafter, Shakeel - codename for the neighbouring company commander, also fetched up. Haider had decided to use the road and reached the place using a Mine Protected Vehicle (MPV). The road came through village Bakiakar. The people of the village were quite used to the vehicle as it was the only means of connecting an outpost of Shakeel's company to the rest of the battalion by road. Suddenly, there were far too many people on the small hill. However, it was due west of the area of interest and this late in the evening with the sun setting behind the hill, visibility of the area of interest from the hill top was great. The area of interest was well lit as seen from the hill top with the sun behind the observers on the hill. Whereas, for anyone looking towards the hill from the area of interest, the hill top would appear hazy with the sun falling directly in their eyes.

"Was it Haider's wisdom again to have chosen such a point?", I thought.

The pleasantries done for the meeting, it was time for me to share my experience of the morning. I got to the point straightaway and shared what I thought was the point where the sound originated from. Interestingly, as in the case of Sodal, the exact place on the ridge above the slope where I thought the point was, stood a villager in a red T-shirt. No plausible reason for his presence could be figured out. He was perched on the table top where one side of it sloped into the pond area and the other sloped towards village Bakiakar. A clear look out man. His bright red T-shirt reflected the sunlight well. The point was immediately christened 'area red' - and that is how half the codewords were invented in any case.

Haider decided that two teams from my company will cordon off the area pond from the north and east, whereas three teams of Shakeel will lay cordon from the west and south. I was to lead search into the area while Haider's team would be in reserve. Haider also decided that the operation will be launched on the morning of the day after next to allow for a cooling off period.

Such meetings were the kind that commanders in field look forward to, since it was difficult to find company of fellow officers in the field on daily basis. These meetings were typically better still for the tea and light snacks that were savoured during the meeting. Tea of course was carried in insulated, thermos flasks from base itself. Sometimes, a refreshing glass of 'nimboo pani' was used to good effect, especially in the summer months. It was also way more refreshing. The boss used such opportunities to treat his team leaders to classy snacks since he had access to better cooks in the battalion HQ.

The meeting was over by 6 PM and the teams started their journeys back to their respective bases. I had again decided to avoid the jungle. The team returned pretending to be a curfew enforcement patrol in the evening. Once in, I briefed my 'O' group about the impending operation. However, there were a good thirty hours to launch. I checked the interception logs and was relieved to not hear any mention of the morning incident. On a separate note, a group of G series militants were gearing up to meet around the time. Place and time, however, was all in code and not discernible.

I went to bed anxiously. The next twenty-four hours were going to be difficult to pass. Such is the soldier leader's dilemma. To go out into an operation is what a soldier longs for given the years of training but at the same time, the leader is busy thinking through and preparing for any and every eventuality that might occur. The soldier leader has to above all prepare for each of these contingencies mentally and put together material where required physically.

The following day went into fine tuning the preparations for the operation to be launched at night. Special emphasis was once again on communication and coordination. This time the cordoning was to happen in the jungle and that too at night. A codeword had been decided to be used to identify own people at night. It was specially required to marry up with other teams in the cordon at night. Fratricide was not the least welcome. I had spent time separately with my own team working on the coordination and drills required for the search. By the evening, everything was in order, the team confident and looking forward to the operation. I too had decided to retire early in order to wake up at 1 AM - my usual sleeping time on other days. It was beginning to get dark.

I had barely settled in my room when my phone began to ring. It was a line call from my no. 2 platoon sentry. No. 2 platoon sentry manned the post over looking the 'chor rasta' and could see in the general direction of the Bakiakar forest.

"Saheb! You have to see towards Bakiakar forest! There is a bright light above the horizon on the forest.", said the sentry.

I ran outside and looked towards the forest. The forest was all dark and the entire outline of the forest forming the horizon was lit in a warm lining- as if things were on fire. I was still trying to figure out what had happened when my phone began to ring again. This time it was a call from Haider.

"Maqbool! We will have to call off the operation in the morning. The neighbouring battalion launched an operation earlier in the day today and trapped six militants - all G series, inside a house of which they had confirmed information. They were all holed up inside a hideout right above the hearth in the house. When the fire fight broke out, the gas cylinder in the kitchen burst leading to a massive fire in the house. Fire brigade has been pressed into action and they have managed to contain the fire just to that house. I guess we have missed our target by a whisker.", said Haider.

"Roger sir! No wonder we were trying to figure out the unusual lighting above the forest horizon here. It's a massive bad luck sir!".

Haider hung up and I was immediately disappointed. I was so looking forward to it. It's a rarity that one gets to go on a hunt in the jungles these days.

"Should I have engaged yesterday?", as a question was going to haunt me for a few days to come. But before that, I had an operation to be called off - a massive disappointment for every soldier. I decided to go to the village the next morning with my team nevertheless.

Even before I left next morning, the radio intercepts had confirmed six of the G series were in the house at village Bakiakar. The militant tanzeem - LeT was praying for them. The entire LeT leadership consisting of G3, G5, G6, G7, G8 and G9 had been roasted in the house of which only charred remains were left. Six badly burnt AK-47s with magazines had been recovered in the house. The company commander who had conducted the operation had sat through the night waiting for the fire to douse itself and for it to be day. The operation had been hugely successful. G2 was the new LeT commander in north Kashmir now as he had received sudden elevation with the entire intervening hierarchy wiped out in a single blow. The officer leading the operation was a fearless Sikh from Amritsar who was soon to be decorated for gallantry with a Sena medal. It was he who had figured out the well concealed hideout. For the purpose, he took internal and external measurements of all the rooms in the house - a stroke of genius for the hideout was built into the mezzanine above the ground and was very difficult to locate. The firefight had lasted for a very brief period of time - thanks to the gas cylinder going off - a divine intervention indeed. None of the boys were hurt in the operation. A situation for a happy post operation sit rep[18].

The militants of course had gotten together for a meeting and many a codewords being used suddenly became clear. Of course, they were also not going to be used again. The militants were operating out of the village and the forest in area pond with no fixed pattern as such for hiding out of in the area.

I came back ruing the missed chance. If only I had a bigger team the day prior. But fate is always predestined. Perhaps there were not all six present at the point the previous day. I could only console myself. I looked at my team and they did not appear half as disappointed as me. I, however, was.

"Am I attaching far too much personal equity to the situation? Perhaps standing back at that point in time, I would have still not chosen to engage." I suddenly felt better. "You need to leave a few things to the Gods above!" But at the same time, I hated missed opportunities.

The next couple of days passed rather slowly. I often re-lived the morning patrol and how things could have been done differently. The militants' radio networks were suddenly quiet in the area. Of course, it was going to take time for the G series to resurface. Most of their radio sets were in any case burnt in the fire. It was also learnt through radio intercepts how G2 and G4 had narrowly escaped the

____

[18] short for situational report

other day as they were yet to join the meeting before the operation started. Further, G2 and G4 were known to operate further to the east and rarely crossed this side. Beg was the only one who surfaced regularly on the radio net now. There had been serious setbacks for the militant tanzeems. They were hard pressed to retaliate but were also on the back foot. The only clear voice that remained in the area belonged to Beg and Beg was under tremendous pressure now. I assumed that the developments in general would have created significant pressures on the OGWs and the sympathisers in the area.

7

Lady Luck smiles again!

The area had become pretty boring suddenly with nearly no action happening anywhere. The radio networks were mostly quiet. No breakthrough seemed to be anywhere close. I was looking hard for the next clue to work on. Even the local information coming in only talked about the occasional cross movement of militants. I was finding it hard to pass the long summer days. However, things were going to change rather quickly.

One fine Sunday in July, when I had consigned to the fact that this was going to be another one of those boring days, I was informed of an unlikely visitor to the op base. I had long since given up on him. Hence, I was surprised to learn that Riyaz had come calling. I asked for Riyaz to be brought up to the meeting room. The meeting room for civilian visitors was more of a dark room that could make anyone sitting in it for a while, nervous. It was a six feet by four feet box, so designed that at least one of the guards could keep an eye on the visitor but the visitor could not see anything outside just in case someone was trying to better understand the base layout. Now Riyaz sat in it, his hands fidgety, anxiously waiting for me.

"How are you? We finally get to meet again.", I said entering the the wooden box.

"Jai Hind Saheb! How are you?", replied Riyaz.

"It is good to meet you after such a long time. What kept you?", I asked.

"I have information on the one man everyone is looking for - Mohd. Ayub Khan.", said Riyaz.

I had actually all but forgotten about Ayub in the wake of all the other action that had been happening. Getting the G-series would have been prestigious and missing the opportunity naturally had me disappointed. But Ayub was way bigger. The oldest surviving head of HM - the man who mobilised the funds locally to sustain the tanzeem. But at the same-time, there were political implications of apprehending Ayub. Ayub was known to be well connected. Further, he was in a neighbouring area. By day, venturing into a neighbouring area and conducting such a high profile operation would not go unnoticed.

I decided to apprise Haider of the situation. A plan was quickly formulated and Haider took on the responsibility of coordinating with the neighbouring battalions.

I knew operating by day is extremely difficult and in this case where the target was of such profile, there were sure to be people on the lookout. The element of surprise was the key, else the target could easily slip away. The one thing in my favour was that Riyaz knew the exact house where the target was.

I ordered my team to prepare for the lightening strike - a newly coined codeword between me and my team. The team was ready to leave within 15 minutes. Once again a local Sumo, plying as a taxi on the road outside had been impounded and vacated of its passengers. In less than 5 minutes, the Sumo was occupied with my team and Riyaz, with me on the wheel. I began briefing my team on the move in the vehicle. In less than 10 minutes, the vehicle was halted by me at a desolate place short of getting out of my own area. The team now quickly pulled out the burkhas and each one wore one, including me. There was a spare one for Riyaz - after all his identity needed protection the most. Even though it was rare for women clad in burkhas to drive a Sumo in Kashmir, I decided to take my chances. The vehicle was yet again on full throttle heading towards the target village. The timing of the operation was somehow spot on. The down military convoy had passed by and the up convoy was a good three hours away, implying comparative ease of movement on the roads without any bottle necks. Plus, Army was yet again rarely known to launch operations at such a time so the surveillance by the militants' elements would have been low too. Unhindered move allowed for my team to reach the target village in less than forty five minutes.

I halted the vehicle at the entrance to the target house. Half the team had been directed to immediately move and cover the rear of the house to cutoff any escape routes. Two members of the team covered the front entrance, while I and my best scout entered the house. The team had yet again managed to achieve complete surprise. Those in the house were shocked to see my team. And I was surprised to see Ayub sitting in the middle of the house - very very relaxed. He made no attempt whatsoever to escape or even put up a fight. Yet again it took me a few seconds to recover from the situation. Unexpected outcomes have the ability to paralyse action.

As soon as I came to my senses, Ayub was nabbed and put into the rear of the vehicle. Riyaz had already provided a positive identification. The team had quickly mounted the vehicle as soon as I had reversed it. I carried out a quick check that everyone was in and stepped on the accelerator. A revolver had been recovered on Ayub that further confirmed that the person picked up was indeed a negative element. I was disappointed for the lack of fight put up by Ayub. However, Ayub appeared supremely confident and in complete control of his emotions.

I dropped Riyaz enroute at a suitable place and called Haider on the cell phone and received further instructions. Haider had anticipated that there may be some trouble created by Ayub's supporters in Handwara town, so it would be best if Ayub is taken to the nearest battalion HQ under whose jurisdiction the village where he was arrested fell. I carried out the orders.

At the neighbouring battalion HQ, Ayub was now brought in and his interrogation by a host of agencies began. Ayub was that high profile. Ayub surprisingly appeared relaxed and calm throughout the interrogation. When the interrogation was finally over and Ayub's identity established beyond doubt, Ayub demanded that he be allowed to speak with certain senior ministers in the state cabinet. The ministers when contacted promptly washed their hands off him claiming they had nothing to do with him. Surprisingly, he next wanted to speak with those in the central government. That is when Ayub realised, he had been orphaned. His confidence and calmness gave way to an instant insecurity and he finally broke down and began to cry. Repentance often hits first in such cases as until then, the hangover of power he enjoyed had him intoxicated. Ayub had no one to save him now and he was too high profile to be left alone. Ayub was, therefore, suitably removed from the situation in north Kashmir.

Going by his popularity, Haider had expected an instant backlash. He knew the word would spread and anything was possible. The battalion was, therefore, given orders to ensure safety and security above everything else. Operations were to be kept to the bare minimum. This went on for nearly a month. But nothing really happened. The radio networks discussed and mourned Ayub's death but no one had the courage to retaliate. The militant tanzeems were well and truly on the back foot now. Losses in recent times had piled up for both HM and LeT.

I was personally happy at an individual level. The missed chance in Bakiakar was behind me now. The team couldn't have been in higher spirits. The parties with Akbar were only getting better. The friendship had evolved to a level where we were now discussing about making a weekend trip to Gulmarg with some of his good friends especially of the opposite sex. I enjoyed keeping the talking to purely the fantasy stage. Strictly not to be materialised.

I, however, was amazed at the freedom that Kashmiri women in the burkha enjoyed - the level to which they were willing to explore under the burkha. Burkha provided a certain level of security through anonymity that perhaps a woman without burkha did not enjoy in a conservative society. A clear identity in the open was way more restrictive. In an otherwise conservative Muslim majority society in Kashmir, the burkha was all about emancipation. I, however, was disinclined to explore that any further, definitely not at the risk to my life. What if someone did to me, what I had done to Ayub under a burkha?

In the one month since the Ayub episode, Riyaz had completely disappeared - not even a phone call since. I refrained from calling him much. It was best not to establish any contact to conceal the informer's identity. Riyaz too evaded the temptation to seek any reward for the information. Thankfully, he was not hard pressed for money, his job with the Territorial Army (TA) looked after him financially. I, however, wondered why Riyaz would do such a thing? What was his motivation if he did not want even a financial reward? He could not even brag about it. He could neither tell his friends for the sake of his life. He could not tell even other military personal for they would get after him for not giving them the high profile kill in the first place. And above all, why had he chosen to help me? The question intrigued me.

"I will ask him when we meet next.", I thought.

Most radio stations by now had disappeared from the area. If anything, one could only hear those who survived in other adjoining areas. The only strong transmissions that remained belonged to Beg. And Beg was under tremendous pressure. He had the added responsibility of recruiting new cadres for the militant tanzeems. The pressure to find the informers remained on him.

On one of the routine returns from daytime patrolling, I again found Ayaz on the road passing through the biggest village in my area - Shehlal. I remembered meeting him earlier in Sodal. So, I asked him to accompany me back to my op base while engaging him in a conversation. Ayaz was more than happy doing so. I could sense Ayaz really didn't have anything else to do.

"What are you doing here?", I asked.

"I was just visiting an old friend in Shehlal.", replied Ayaz.

I was impressed with the casual manner in which Ayaz engaged with me. Not many in the area could do that. Most became nervous when spoken to by me - the local Company Commander. I used to enjoy the higher status.

"I remember having met you earlier in Sodal.", I said. "You are Ayaz."

"Yes Saheb! That is right.", acknowledged Ayaz.

By this time my team had arrived at the op base and I chose to bring Ayaz in. I sensed Ayaz was upto something and I needed to know or at the least try and figure out.

Ayaz was now seated in the meeting room where I met all such visitors. The meeting room failed to have the desired effect on Ayaz. He remained calm.

"I do not often see people floating around much in other villages as much as you do.", I remarked. "Most friends here prefer to meet outside in towns like Handwara. Seeing you in Sodal the other day and now in Shehlal cannot be plain coincidence."

"Actually sir! I keep floating around in the area. I am in close contact with the company commander Saheb in Magam and he knows me well.", said Ayaz.

"I will speak to Shakeel about it when I meet him next." Shakeel was the Magam company commander's pseudo name. "But it still does not explain your presence in Shehlal."

"Sir! I act as his source. Hence, I keep moving around to gather information."

That was the first time anyone had ever made an open claim to being an informer.

"Do you understand that if you are moving around gathering information in my area and passing it on to my neighbouring Company Commander, it may have an adverse impact on my reputation with my boss?", I said.

"But Saheb! I am told that Magam is the headquarters under which all this area also lies.", replied Ayaz.

"That is true but for Haider not Shakeel.", I countered. "Make sure that any information you may have about my area is passed on to me as well."

"Saheb! I assure you that. In the past, I have shared some information about militants but Shakeel was unable to get any result. With you I may actually be successful. After all, I get rewarded only when there is a successful mission. I am glad that I may get a chance to work with you. I have heard a lot from the locals about your style of conducting operations.", said Ayaz.

I didn't know how to react to the flattery. Being a good actor that I was, I chose to not react whatsoever. I also didn't know what to make of it. I chose to let Ayaz go but only after exchanging cell phone numbers. Ayaz confessed that his cell phone was sponsored by Haider and only his largesse allowed him to afford one. I was going to do a cross check on him anyway. My sixth sense told me that Ayaz may pass on some information to me in the future. I could sense that Ayaz had no real job and depended on such activities for his survival. I remembered that Ayaz was a surrendered militant and perhaps, therefore, knew whom to keep a tab on in the area.

Shakeel confirmed knowing Ayaz but did not find him of any significant value. He confirmed receiving tidbits of information from Ayaz but most, rather all of it was not actionable. I thanked Shakeel as I was happy to get the confirmation on Ayaz. I was happy to learn that Ayaz spent most of his time preoccupied with gathering information. With a little encouragement Ayaz could indeed be useful.

And useful he was. For, from the very next day he started calling and reporting events in Magam. Most of it was insignificant and not of use to me. But that Ayaz was making an effort, was visible.

After numerous inconsequential calls, I awaited some actionable information. And it came. Rather it was really not much of an actionable information, but it was information nevertheless.

On a lazy Sunday morning yet again, while I was in the mood to relax and chill it out, Ayaz called, nearly a month after the meeting in Shehlal. It was 10 AM and I was still in my track suit after the morning fitness routine. Ayaz informed having spotted a HM militant who was known to be operating in Rajwar area and was seen in broad daylight passing through the main marketplace in Magam. He was on the internal road and Ayaz started to follow him. The militant - Mansoor, decided to climb the hill onto one side of the road which had village Sodal on the other side and if one continued on that path, one would generally be heading towards Rajwar forest where Mansoor was known to operate. So, Ayaz guessed that Mansoor was headed towards village Chak Sodal and since it was in my area of responsibility, he chose to call me.

I was double minded. It was broad daylight and moving out was sure to attract attention. Additionally, I knew that Mansoor could very easily melt into the wilderness given the direction he was headed in. Besides, just beyond Chak Sodal lay a small forest and Mansoor knew the area well. Hence, spotting him and catching him was going to be a really low probability bet. To add to that, I had no means of identifying the target.

However, at the same time, receiving real time first hand information is rare and Ayaz was providing one for the first time. I felt compelled to act simply to keep Ayaz motivated. The decision taken, I ordered my team to get ready to move. Time was of essence here. I quickly changed into battle gear. The 'putty parades'[19] at NDA came in handy. Eight of my QRT were ready in no time and were at the gate. The guard at the gate had been asked to flag down a Sumo. When I reached the gate, the Sumo had already been stopped but the passengers were reluctant to get down. After all, on a Sunday, the frequency of available public transport is quite low. I had to resort to screaming on the people making them get down in a hurry and vacate the vehicle. I was well within my rights to impound a vehicle for military duty. The team quickly mounted and left. The guards at the gate were going to take care of the stranded passengers.

The situation was such that things could have gone wrong. There was no clear plan as such. I had decided to make a quick vehicle based patrol in my area given the chances of bumping into the militant were bleak. Further, I just did not know the target. I underestimated Ayaz though.

Ayaz in the meantime, hitched a ride from Magam to just short of my op base. As soon as I had started from the op base, Ayaz flagged me down. I quickly took Ayaz

---

[19] Timed practice drills undertaken to change dresses quickly as a means of training to drive home discipline and punctuality.

onboard. One of the team members took off his shirt and gave it to Ayaz and another gave his 'patka'[20] that was enough to conceal Ayaz's identity inside the vehicle. I was happy with Ayaz's initiative. That alone had increased the probability of success significantly. I now briefed the team on the move. The plan was simple. If Mansoor is spotted, the team was to quickly alight and cover him. If Mansoor opens up, the fire was to be returned else Mansoor was to be arrested. Things were moving really fast. I had barely finished my briefing, and the vehicle had just about crossed village Shehlal. Everyone looked at the team with surprise. As we emerged on the other side of the ridge separating Sodal and Shehlal, Ayaz spotted Mansoor. Mansoor though had originally given people an impression that he was headed for Chak Sodal but had come back onto the Shehlal road thereby creating a ruse. But his luck had run out and mine was in top gear.

The vehicle had barely crossed Mansoor and gone 50 meters past, when I hit the brakes and brought the vehicle to a halt. The team popped out and took cover on either side of the road. I stepped out leaving Ayaz in the vehicle. Mansoor stood frozen as if a hare would in bright headlights on a dark night. Mansoor was accompanied by another man. Following the two at a distance of about ten meters was the other man's wife wearing a burkha. I did not know but then she helped by stopping automatically

---

[20] a piece of cloth used to cover one's face and neck usually of black or Olive Green colour in the Army.

alongside her husband. She could have very easily made the getaway.

Mansoor was like no other militant I had seen before. Very well groomed, clean shaven and handsome looking fair guy dressed in a red T-shirt and blue jeans and wearing Nike sneakers. Clearly there was no weapon on him or his accomplice. As I approached Mansoor, Mansoor began to tremble in fear as a last lone dry leaf on a tree in autumn in Kashmir suddenly subjected to a cold windy storm would. I was nearly sure that I had got my man but in the absence of a weapon the doubts remained.

The sneaker laces made of nylon came in handy as those were used to tie down the militant - a quick improvisation given the lack of planning. A search of the militant and his accomplice was quickly carried out. The search yielded nothing incriminating. The woman of course could not be searched in the absence of a lady constable. It was thus decided to take the arrested personal to Magam. For the purpose, another Sumo coming down the same road was impounded. Some passengers in the Sumo cursed their luck for the second time running. I assured them that the Sumo will return for them in fifteen minutes. Ayaz and Mansoor and his accomplices could not have been allowed to mix.

The lady was asked to occupy the co-driver's seat in the second Sumo while I figured out who sits where and how to secure the target. This is when one of the boys raised an alarm. Gurung had been keeping an eye on the lady surreptitiously. The lady when she thought she had a chance of going unspotted, sitting in the vehicle, was trying to slip something away. This is what Gurung picked up. She had been trying to stow something away under the vehicle seat. It was a pistol - a 9mm Browning wrapped in a piece of cloth. Clearly it belonged to Mansoor and she had been entrusted with carrying it under the burkha. She knew if the same is recovered on her person, she could be in trouble. She was in trouble now.

I was relieved. The discovery of the pistol put to rest all doubts. I could now, on radio, inform Haider of the successful operation. The two vehicles then took off for Magam. The entire operation was over in forty-five minutes. The action was sudden and so surprising for Mansoor that he had had no time to react. By the time he got his wits about him, he was already under arrest. I picked up a desolate spot on the way and let Ayaz go.

At the Magam base, Haider along with his Adjutant received my team. He was happy and so was the team. The Adjutant was particularly happy for he would once again have something substantial to report in his daily sitrep to the higher headquarters. Things had luckily gone well for me. Over the next ten days, detailed interrogation of Mansoor was carried out. People came pouring from neighbouring areas to interrogate him and identify him. Mansoor divulged precious little of use. If anything, it was previously known to the forces. An absence of cooperation and repentance from Mansoor compelled the forces to suitably remove him from the situation in North Kashmir. Mansoor's accomplices too were handed over to the police to be released into the environment. Clearly they were headed for Shehlal that day, which confirmed to me that Shehlal really was the epicentre of all activity in my area.

Most importantly, Ayaz had become a close confidant of mine. He was suitably rewarded with money over numerous followup secret meetings with me. Another lesson I had learnt was to split the reward money into small packets over a longer duration rather than just one big pay out. That kept Ayaz interested. Additionally, it kept him away from making a sudden large spend and thus, getting noticed.

A day after the apprehension, Beg once again reported the arrest of Mansoor in great detail. I heard it all and was surprised to learn of the details that Beg knew. But then the entire operation had been conducted in broad daylight with people working in the fields nearby. Additionally, Mansoor's accomplices were alive and released to the environment. Beg had the means to learn of it all.

The Gods had been kind to me. Had I been delayed by five minutes, Mansoor would have hit the patch of the road passing through the narrow forest. Mansoor could have taken his chances of making a run and in the absence of any firing from Mansoor, I would have found it difficult to shoot Mansoor. Chasing him with battle gear would have been tough. Kashmiris are really fit to outrun anyone in the mountains. Conversely, had I been five minutes early, I would have made the turn on the road to Chak Sodal and again completely missed Mansoor. But then, what is the point in discussing what did not happen! God had been kind, especially to Ayaz too. The monetary award kept him going as the only primary source of income. This breakthrough had secured him a temporary financial stability besides encouraging him. He was thankful to me that I had acted on his input. Without the action, nothing worthwhile would have happened.

My team and Haider were both happy. The battalion was moving along, realising its objectives especially when all the other company areas appeared dull and quiet.

Nothing keeps the morale of the men higher than success at regular intervals and nothing keeps them happier than being busy and meaningfully employed. I was managing to do both. The men were living through and developing stories they were going to tell for a long time to come.

Beg was being interrogated yet again, admonished even on the recent happenings and all the more so since it was believed to have happened right under his nose. Yet again, Beg did not know about the source of information. He conjectured that it was a lucky catch by me. This was a relief for me since I understood that no-one suspected the involvement of any source.

I was back to handling company's internal affairs which were already mostly well sorted. The administration needed to be looked into everyday. And of course, the daily visitors were still coming in, in good number. Also, the good times with Akbar continued and he had profanities in store for people who harboured militants. I always wondered why nothing ever came out of the village Shehlal.

The Mansoor episode had not even died down completely that I again received a call from Ayaz. Somehow, it was again 10AM in the morning. Half the manpower in the op base was already committed and out of the base on routine duties. This time too the information involved village Khan Sodal. There was definitive information of presence of four hardcore militants of HuJI staying in the village. They were transiting and were temporarily halted in Khan Sodal for the day. Khan Sodal was comparatively a small village. I quickly appreciated the situation. I could muster three teams including my own QRT from the camp. I needed at least two more teams - one each from neighbouring camps to carry out an effective cordon and search operation. I ordered for the three teams to be prepared and gathered behind the buildings offering no visual to anyone looking into the base. Simultaneously, I requested for and was granted one team each from the neighbouring C & D companies. I knew that once again, I was mobilising the teams in broad daylight. Since Sodal was in my area, any of the teams moving towards Sodal from my op base will lead to the Early Warning elements alerting the OGWs in the area. Hence, the movement had to be swift.

D company team, however, could not be vehicle bound in the absence of any roads in their area but was best poised to reach Sodal undetected since the route came through a forest with no habitation enroute. I made my plans and conveyed the same to everyone. D company team was to move out first on foot. I had anticipated it would take the team about 20 minutes to reach. The rest of the teams would be vehicle bound and reach the village as quickly as they can and lay a cordon. Since all this was to happen by day, there were clearly no major coordination issues. D company team would cut off the village from the forest side. My own two teams would cordon from the east and north whereas C company team would cordon the village from the west. I had anticipated that when the D company team reaches Sodal and if the word reaches the militants, the militants would try to make a dash for village Batpura that was downhill and across the paddy fields from Sodal. I, thus decided to move with my team in advance on the outer road and move into Sodal from village Batpura as soon as the team from D company reaches Sodal. The D company team was instructed to inform arrival accordingly. I also realised that moving my team to Batpura would set up a ruse for anyone who may be on the lookout.

Once again civil vehicles were impounded for the task. A Sumo for me and my QRT. A minibus for the other two teams. I was to control the operation on radio.

I left first with my team on the outer road. I knew it did not directly lead to Sodal and hence, no one would be alarmed. It would be a routine movement to battalion headquarters at Magam. The vehicle was stopped near village Batpura and the team alighted. I awaited communication from the D company team lead. The other two teams plus one from C company too had left on vehicles ten minutes after me. As soon as, the D company team leader reported in position, my team entered village Batpura to cross over and walk across the paddy fields to Sodal. Within five minutes, the remaining three teams also confirmed an 'in location' report. I was expecting the D company team to have given that report a little earlier than they did. But nothing seemed out of place. The cordon was effectively in place and there were no gaps. Just when I was planning on the next move, I was surprised to see two vehicles of the police, with the armed special operations group, lead by their maverick inspector - Sajid arriving on the scene. It was already noon.

I met inspector Sajid, who I knew through my liaison visits to the Handwara police station. I was surprised to learn that they too had the same information that I had. Sajid and his team were located in Handwara and had their sources. I was happy to learn of the information getting corroborated. But, I was also alarmed to see the way it was spreading. I sensed that the local population must hate these set of militants for the information to spread the way it was or the militants were lackadaisical in the way they operated for many locals to know about their presence. Incidentally, within minutes, I learnt that Haider was on his way too. He too now knew something about the militants it seemed.

Haider arrived within fifteen minutes of the information of his arrival. By then, the crackdown had been announced and the local population gathered. Somehow, the people appeared quite relaxed and there were no tell tale signs whatsoever. The plan for the house to house search was being formulated when Haider spoke to me.

"What is the information?"

"Sir! The information is of presence of four hardcore militants in the village.", I replied.

"Alright! As per digital intelligence received from an intercepted call at the higher headquarters in Srinagar, the militants last identified their location to their handlers across. They claimed to be hiding inside the masjid in village Batpura. They claimed to have escaped thanks to a tip off by Beg just in time.", apprised Haider.

"But sir! I have confirmed information which is corroborated by the police SOG as well.", I replied. "Could it be that they got the village name wrong? Shall we search inside the masjid in this village?"

"Alright! But let's make it quick."

I had never entered a masjid in complete battle gear before. I was worried about the sensibilities of the common people. Raiding a place of religious importance was never talked about or even taught in any training establishment. Then it occurred to me that I could get inspector Sajid's team to do so. I had the right options in place luckily.

The search of the masjid was still on when one of the teams in road opening party near Batpura reported that when their vehicle had stopped on the road, there was a general uneasiness amongst the people and few had even shrieked and run away. They were incidentally very close to the spot where my team had halted just before cutting across to Sodal. This confirmed that something was actually wrong in Batpura. Perhaps, my appreciation was right after all that if the militants had to run, they would towards Batpura. In the meantime, the search of the masjid had yielded nothing. I informed Haider and decided to shift the focus on to Batpura.

I directed my teams to upstick and move onto cordoning Batpura. As the teams moved, I had to release the people back into the village and quickly obtain the NOC. Not to be left out of the action, I quickly wound things up in Sodal and moved to join the teams in Batpura. Inspector Sajid left for Handwara with his team not knowing what was happening.

I had barely joined Haider near the masjid in Batpura, when Haider again received a message of interception of the militants' next phone call. The Digital intelligence team had locked on to the militant's cellphone. They had already shifted from Batpura and had reported that they were now safe in Haji Saheb's house in the next village - Khanpura as they had nearly been trapped by the forces. I quickly ordered that a few locals be taken along and Haji's house be identified and be cordoned off.

The target house happened to be in the next village in line with Batpura. By the time the teams were finally in place, it was already 5.45 PM. I quickly inspected the cordon. The target house was the southernmost house in the village - a three storied house that was palatial given the general standard of houses in the village. This corner of the village was in effect a cluster of four houses separated by a small track running through the village. The target house was the biggest of the four with a large compound all around it completely devoid of any vegetation or cover.

A smaller two storied house was immediately next to it to its north sharing a common boundary wall. To its east, was an old dilapidated house made of wood. On the corner, between the two neighbouring houses was another two storied house that was relatively newly built - the walls were yet to be plastered. The southern side of the target house was barricaded with a tall wall beyond which was a slope that eventually led to a river further south just about 50 meters from the compound wall. The intervening piece of land was heavily silted with no underbrush that would mostly flood in summers when the rains came or in winters during heavy snow. There was very little cover so the teams in cordon sat behind thin trees. I ordered them to retreat backwards and use one of the embankments of the river as protection against any fire from the militants.

By the time the cordon was adjusted, the village had already emptied itself without the forces making a request to do so. This was a clear sign of militant presence. In the absence of any civil population, it became difficult to carry out an effective search operation. With great difficulty, two people were caught and brought forward to accompany the forces for the search as witnesses. I had to lead the search operation.

I quickly formulated a plan. Clearly, the militants were well behind cover and not likely to change houses under observation of the forces. I realised that the target was cut off only from the south and in case of contact, the militants could easily escape towards the north into the rest of the village. Clearing each house then, would come at a heavy cost.

I decided to guard against this. Haider discussed the situation with me and I apprised Haider of what I was thinking. Haider further thought that from the militants' perspective, they would be best off holing up inside the Haji's large house. The house would provide them with maximum protection in an operation. I informed Haider that I would first clear the other 3 houses in the cluster and install our team members as stops to ensure the militants cannot escape from this cluster of houses. Once effectively surrounded, we would search the Haji's house. Haider agreed.

It was already quite late now and night fall was an hour away. Sunlight was already gone. I decided to search the easternmost house first. I along with my half team of six began the search operation. Two of the six stayed outside covering the main door of the house. The two scouts, I and my buddy entered the house. While one buddy pair entered one of the rooms, the other stayed outside the room covering the other. Within the room, while one searched, his buddy covered him. All the rooms were quickly flushed out. The flushing out started with the lower floors and finished on the top. There was no time for a detailed search which otherwise would have started from the top. There was nothing incriminating to suggest a more thorough search. On clearance, I got six members of Haider's QRT to occupy the first floor of the house and maintain a dominating cover over the target house and the old wooden house next to it. I then proceeded to clear the remaining two storied house to the north of the target house.

My team entered the next house compound and found a barn in the corner which I decided to clear first. It was eerily quiet in the village. One could only hear my voice every now and then giving out instructions or an occasional cow mooing in some house upset for having been left alone in the evening. The barn was searched first and found clear. The two storied house was to be flushed next. The house as anticipated was clear. I stationed six of my team members in the house. I then headed back to the old wooden house to the east of the target house.

I was accompanied by an old man from the village- the only one the team could find, for the search operation. He always went into the house first before my team made the intervention. He was now going into the wooden house. The old man quickly entered the ground floor rooms and then took an external staircase to the first floor. He soon came back to report the house was clear. As he came out, he just stepped on to a side and stood next to the staircase signalling all clear. My team stepped forward for the search. As soon as the scouts and I neared the open verandah in front of the rooms on the ground floor, we first took cover behind whatever we could find before storming the rooms. I was behind a very narrow wooden pillar.

We had not anticipated to find anyone in this old rag of a house. But as I looked up, I was shocked. Two of the militants were hiding in the ground floor room right opposite. It must have been a fraction of a second over which I and the first of the militants made eye contact. The militant was already ready to fire and he did. The militant was ready beforehand and had acquired his target while my weapon was still pointing towards the ground. Those two militants inside the room opened fire simultaneously engaging me and one of the scouts at the same time. Luckily for me, nothing hit me. At just three meters from the militant, the very narrow pillar had saved me. My luck was indeed on my side.

I now returned fire. Thankfully, the six member team of Haider's QRT was well located to engage the militants from the first house we had cleared. As they opened fire, they shot one on the spot and injured the second. There were in reality two more militants hiding outside. The other two militants also opened fire now. It was then that I noticed that there was a passageway in the middle of the two ground floor rooms which lay concealed until then. The passage led into the Haji's house behind, which the two able bodied and the one injured militant took to move out of the wooden house.

The militants now ran through the open lawn in front of the haji's house, firing on both sides. Luckily, this was that one percent occurrence where the house boundary walls were made of bricks. No one was injured. The bullets fired by the militants either hit the walls or flew overhead. The three remaining militants had entered the triple storied large house and locked themselves in. Thankfully, they could not have escaped further.

It was now suddenly deafeningly silent again. Even I was not speaking then. It is also then that I realised that one of the scouts had been hit by the militant's opening salvo. One bullet had entered from the side and exited the soldier's body. He was bleeding but looked in control. He had taken evasive action and jumped to one side and taken cover before any more damage could be done. His buddy and I quickly dragged him backwards. He was given first aid and put into a vehicle for the nearest medical aid post. In less than an hour, he was in expert hands. Luckily for him, the bullet had missed hitting anything critical - no organs, not even the backbone. He was going to be alright in three months time.

Everyone had now frozen. It had suddenly become dark. The search had to be suspended until the morning. However, the cordon had to be strengthened. Accordingly, Haider called for additional troops and a Mine Protected Vehicle (MPV).

At around 8 PM, the militants tried breaking the cordon, but were effectively challenged by my half team in the other two-storied house. The militants retreated into the Haji's house. It was quiet once again. The dead body of one of the militants lay hanging half out of the room resting on the wooden window sill. There were three more and one of them was injured, holed up in the Haji's house. I moved around as best I could given that it was dark and people could have been jittery. I continued to guide the additional teams coming in to lay the cordon.

The villagers did not return that night. I wondered where they went in such situations. The long wait for the morning began. The night itself suddenly became longer in the absence of light. We had to restrict to darkness for we did not want to give away our location to the militants. It was now a guessing game and concealing information helped.

I had been now mentally alert and on my feet for twelve straight hours that had not been as tiring as it was now. I had to stand or stay still and just be attentive in the dark. I and my team had tucked in into the cleared house where my half team already was. The last meal the team had consumed was the breakfast. The radio set batteries had all drained out including the spares. The team was searching for anything to eat in the house. Incidentally, the people of the house had left behind cooked dinner. The team enjoyed bits of 'kadam ka saag' with steamed rice. They felt heavenly. With some food in the tummy, I felt recharged. Of course, not everyone was going to be lucky tonight and many would go without dinner.

Post dinner, the waiting became tougher. It was pitch dark outside. The electricity supply was erratic. It would frequently come and go. In one of the houses, someone had left behind some milk on an electric stove. The burnt milk would start to smell every time the electricity came making someone in the team hungrier. It further happened to be a moon less night.

While it was absolutely quiet, at around 10.30 PM, I was startled to hear loud voices again. The militants had sneaked back through the passage in the wooden house and were trying to break through the cordon. Luckily, the buddy pair right in front were vigilant. They challenged the militants and after a brief exchange of fire, the militants again ran back into the Haji's house. No one was hurt and it became quiet again.

The night was now crawling towards the morning after a brief excitement. For me, the worst time to keep awake was around the time which was my normal sleeping time. And this struggle to stay awake was real. I was alternately trying to lie down flat on my tummy and then sitting up behind cover. In spite of the awkwardness of the position, it was extremely tough to be quiet and awake at the same time. More so, when I was tired operating for more than fifteen hours flat. But that is just what a soldier is trained to do.

The time appeared to pass slowly too. I could not move either, for the fear of giving away my position. And then, I could not let down my team and that thought kept me going through the night. It was a tough night. Every now and then after it would seem like an eternity, when I would see the time, the watch would have barely clocked ten minutes. Time was crawling and so was the night. Thankfully, it was summers and the nights were short. It was now 3 AM and it was to become visibly alright at 5.

"Just two hours to go!", I thought to myself.

But it was not to be! Perhaps the militants thought so as well. They knew that they would be daylighted in another two hours. Hence, their only chance of making a break was now. They believed that more than four hours of quiet would have lulled the Army into lethargy and many may actually be asleep. They finally made an attempt of a daring break. They chose to, this time, jump over the wall to the south of the house towards the river and make a fighting breakout. The forces were thankfully alert. One can expect the Gurkha soldier to be always alert on duty.

What followed was an intense engagement in the pitch dark. I and my team could only watch as the gun battle ensued with the cordon party opposite to us. Lots of gun muzzle flashes and an occasional grenade would go off. It was fireworks. I had no means of finding out which of the flashes were that of the militants in the dark. I and my team, thus chose to not engage. But my other team was in the thick of all the action.

The 3 militants in spite of the heavy exchange of fire managed to cross through the cordon, crossed the river and were now headed in the direction of Sodal. I was clueless as to what had finally happened. My radio set batteries were dead and I was out of communication. The firefight had stopped after an exchange that lasted twenty minutes. It was still dark and no one could move especially now since the firefight had just happened. People could be jittery and shadows could be shot at. I thus, decided to wait for some better visibility. In the meantime, the armoured vehicle that had joined the cordon the previous evening started and left. I was to later learn that one of my boys had received a bullet injury in his right hand. Thankfully rest everyone was alright. In the absence of radio communication, it was getting really frustrating for me.

I thanked God when the visibility improved slightly. I could now move around once again. I chose to do so with my half team. This is when I learnt of the successful break by the militants. I spoke to the other teams for the details. Hearing of what had transpired, I was convinced that some of the militants would have been injured for sure. Time was critical. I figured the injured militants couldn't have gone far. A little more brainstorming allowed me to figure out the probable route they would have taken. It was time to chase and search down every single house on the way.

I had by now called in for additional radio batteries and the communication was back in order. I set out with my team on the path the militants could have taken. The militants had apparently first travelled along the river stream and crossed over using the first bridge to the south on the path to Sodal. My team took the bridge as well. At places now, I could see drops of blood. I sensed I was right. A little down the path was a small group of three houses. The compounds were again barricaded using roofing sheets. The houses had to be searched.

This time we could lay hands on two civilians to accompany for the search. As the civilian boys entered the very first house, they came running back and reported that a militant was in the lawn in front. He was apparently holding a pistol in his hand. I understood that perhaps he was immobile. I and my buddy along with the scouts went around the house and approached the lawn from behind.

From the corner of the house building, I could sense the militant in the lawn. He was writhing in pain. As he saw me peeping from the corner of the house, he threw a grenade at me. The militant was too weak and his attempt landed short. I and my team took evasive action. As the grenade went off, I while still under cover from the corner of the house shot the militant swiftly with a short burst of my AK-47. This militant's story was now over as he was definitely put out of his misery.

As I now took a clear view of the militant, I realised this one was a hardcore - the kind who find it difficult to live in urban areas and who spend most of their time in the jungles. He was kitted up like any militant fighter with pouches. His AK and ammunition was gone perhaps taken along by the others. He had a broken leg at the shin - a bullet had pierced through it. He had perhaps been carried this far. He was left in the lawn with a pistol and a grenade - one in each hand to perhaps offer the last bit of resistance, if discovered. His story was over now.

I informed Haider and had his second team fetch up and take control. I moved on with a word of caution for the second team leader. The militant could still have a primed grenade trapped under him.

Even though, I was nearly convinced that the others perhaps got away for if they were injured too, they would have halted along with the second militant. Nevertheless, I decided to complete the pursuit into Sodal. There were no further tell tale signs, no drops of blood or suggestive looks or give away body language of the locals in Sodal. Things appeared to be normal. I realised that perhaps it made more sense sending in my information sources. I decided to call Ayaz, gave him an update and asked him to get on to the task. I then left. For me, the operation was over. I got on the radio with my signal NCO back at the base and tasked him to scan militant's radio frequencies.

"Find what Beg has to say!", the directions were clear.

It was also time to find the well being of my injured soldiers. They were in good hands and stable in medical terms as I learnt. For them, their respective tenures in the Kashmir Valley were over. Post recuperation and medical leave, they would rejoin their respective parent units. I was to visit them in the hospital soon.

The teams returned to base after more than twenty-four hours out in the field. A sumptuous meal awaited them. For that matter, any good meal after such a long wait always tasted awesome. A soldier gets to taste that more often than any other professional I presume. The operation was a success. No one was fatally or mortally wounded, which was a big relief. One big satisfaction was around how the troops operated in a very flexible and fast changing environment. It was seen by everyone as an evidence of high standards of training. To top it all, the men gave a good account of themselves even when I was out of communication and hence, control for nearly six hours through the night. I felt proud and happy. Very soon the call from Haider's boss came congratulating the team on the success. The team was happy.

Beg was all over the radio that evening. Yet again, he was clueless but under serious pressure. He was unable to explain how the security forces were keeping pace with the militants as they moved from one village to the next. Beg again had no answers except that the militants were careless. The pressure on Beg was immense. I was happy for now - not only the backbone of militants operating in my area was broken, but those transiting through the area were also left not feeling safe. That made me happier. After all, that was my objective like that of any company commander in the valley. I wondered who Beg was though.

The company was well settled in and looking forward to more action and more playing time in the base. There was a general happiness around, which comes from confidence in one's abilities and in this case, it was the entire company that was brimming with confidence. For me, the normal routine again included moving out and meeting people in my area. In other cases, people came calling on me as well. People too looked relaxed or was it my imagination.

8

The retaliation!

I had by now realised that there were two Kashmirs within Kashmir. The vast majority had nothing to do with the militancy in Kashmir. They went about their lives as normally as they could. They were comfortably numb and oblivious to everything around them. They treated the presence of the security forces or that of the militants with the same nonchalance. They went about their professions as best they could - as weavers, land tillers, orchard owners/workers or whatever else they did. For me, it was best to leave them alone and where possible facilitate their business and in the least not do anything to antagonise them in anyway, lest the militants benefit.

The other Kashmir was the one that actively engaged with the militants. Their numbers were small but for them, militancy was business itself - they were busy spreading militant ideology or being affected by it. Anyone who wanted power was surely engaged with the militancy problem. And for some others, it was about just money. The only real problem was that, not one of the locals was openly and vehemently against the militancy in Kashmir or perhaps those were dead already.

And then a few sympathised with them. It was rare the locals stood up by themselves - they were weak and defenceless. But when militant atrocities became too much to handle, they would seek help from the only place help could come with minimum risk - the Indian Army. Though it was strange that most locals referred to the Army as the Indian Army. For them, the Army was as alien as aliens can get. After all, more than 30 years into militancy, the only Hindu population Kashmiris could see was in the uniform. Those who remembered the Kashmiri pundits living in their neighbourhood once, were too old to shape opinions. And those who had seen what happened to Baramulla in 1948 were long since gone. The reality had changed significantly over the years. Now what mattered was what the local madrassas and masjids said. Education can be so corrupting at times.

I, hence, took special care in being sensitive to the feelings of the locals while being just in my dealings with the public. The general public liked me for that. They liked the fact that someone was willing to give them a patient hearing. Maybe sometimes that is all that one wants.

But not everyone was happy with me. Some had been severely offended and held me singly responsible for the wipeout of militants in the area. It was not uncommon for militants to launch an attack on key defence personal. But no one remained in the area to make that happen. Besides, the local population was not against me. In fact, they liked me.

My popularity on account of good behaviour was soaring as was evident from the number of invites I was now receiving for the Iftaar parties for the upcoming Bakr-eid. Things were going smoothly for me. I, however, refused to let things lull me into complacency. In fact, I sensed something could go wrong and was therefore, careful in my day to day management. That I had to be extra careful came as a warning very soon.

It was a mid week morning and one of the senior officers was visiting the battalion headquarters. All officers were required to be present in the headquarters at Magam for which I had planned to leave my op base at 7 AM and make a dash for the headquarters in a gypsy with a very small team. The time was early and the road opening team had not cleared the road yet. I had chosen to take my chances considering this was a one off case and it would be difficult for any wrong elements to predict my move. Hence, I took off with five of my team in a Maruti Gypsy for the battalion headquarters.

There were two roads connecting my op base with Magam. I chose to take the outer longer road. I was driving and fast. I assumed the swiftness of my movement to be a security feature. Most part of the road to Magam was smooth. The first stretch involved coming out of the base, crossing a culvert and emerging out of the line of trees that ran along the stream on which the culvert was. That was followed by a run in the open with paddy fields on either side. As one crossed this stretch that lasted about three kilometres, one would next take a turn left on the road with a long line of villages on one side with Khanpura followed by Batpura and others all the way until Magam. The river behind these villages ran parallel to the road. On the other side, the road ran parallel to a high mountain range, hugging the base of it.

My vehicle had made the turn in less than ten minutes and suddenly came across a patch of road that had mud dumped on it and hence, was rough and I could spot an abandoned tractor trolley occupying most of the road.There was a narrow passage left onto one side of the trolley which the Gypsy would have had to cross in very slow speed. One side of the road had a steep cutting with a fall as the river came very close to the road and the other side rose sharply towards a mountain top. In another minute, I would have been driving through the narrow space left on to one side of the trolley when something struck me. I hit the brakes hard and asked the team to jump out and take cover. I too stepped out with my weapon. I now directed my team to observe carefully and be on the lookout for anyone hiding especially onto the mountain top side.

My team had been in position for nearly ten minutes now. I had to do something. I then chose a likely hiding place for anyone up on the slope and fired a few shots from my weapon in that direction. I was not surprised to receive returning fire. A few short bursts were fired back from the cover of the trees on my team. I was not too off with what I thought could be the spot. There was a large barren steep slope between my team and the line of trees further up on the slope. Moving towards the area where the fire came from was suicidal for it entailed moving upslope at relatively a snail's pace through an open patch on the mountain face. I, therefore, immediately directed a heavier returning fire and called in for additional teams from my op base. The engagement with the militants lasted barely ten minutes after which the militants ran away. No one in my team was hurt. The militants were too far away to have fired on us effectively. The converse was also true. Perhaps they fired back out of frustration. I had two of my team members cross over to the other side of the trolley following a circuitous route to stop all traffic. Surprisingly, there was none coming.

In the meantime, the other teams fetched up and a search of the area started. The militants covering the site were long gone. A thorough search of the site yielded an IED buried into the ground to be activated through a radio signal. It was meant to prevent me from reaching Magam that day or for that matter reaching anywhere at all. I could not reach Magam but was thankfully alive. It was a close shave though.

The same evening I sat celebrating my being alive with a drink while thanking my lucky stars. My brains had worked just in time to prevent what could have been the end of my story. I wondered for long what had prevented the mishap. Was it training or a faint but timely recollection of a similar incident elsewhere where the officer wasn't that lucky. Whatever it was, I and my team were alive and I sat thanking the militant's lack of imagination to come up with something new. I could not afford to be lax and caught off guard again.

That evening I sat listening in to the radio network. Beg only mentioned, "He got away!", during the transmission. That certainly wasn't enough to ascertain but I figured the 'he' could be me. I wondered how they figured I was going to be on the road or was it a general siting to entrap anyone of the security forces. The preparation for the reception of the senior officer had started a little earlier. Though most of it was kept under wraps but perhaps the sprucing up of a helipad at Magam was a give away. The general public could have guessed someone was visiting and in most such cases, all officers gather at the headquarters for a meet up. The road on which I was, was to be used by 2/3 officers that morning. The others had been diverted when I encountered the situation at the site. I figured that the best way to answer was to reconnoiter the other road I could have taken.

The following morning I undertook a foot patrol on the inner road with my team. The aim was to look out for tell tale signs of what could have been an alternate ambush site. Anyone could have figured that I could have only taken one of the two routes available to me that morning. If indeed I was the target, they would have looked to cover both. I was yet again putting up a show that everything was normal. I was a good actor. Not even my own team knew what was going on in my mind. As the team progressed through the villages lined along the road, I interacted as normally with the people as I could. I was trying my best to be casual but at the same time I could sense something amiss. The people interacted with me with a little reservation. They were not the usual free self. They engaged in a manner as if someone under a watch would. I continued to not notice and acted normal.

As my team came clear out of Shehlal, to reach the spot where the team had apprehended Mansoor, I could see a lot of mud that had been freshly dumped as well. The road was elevated with respect to its surroundings. The trolley was of course missing. There was a high ground that separated Shehlal from Sodal, that afforded a dominating view of the spot. The evidence was not entirely conclusive but coupled with villagers' body language confirmed to me that something was indeed wrong. There was no clear logic for the mud to have been dumped at the spot. The pattern was quite similar to the one on the outer road. I also recalled that no civilians were found plying on the road in the morning that the incident had happened. Perhaps, they had been warned to stay off the roads for the day. Perhaps that too explained why the locals were behaving differently.

I spent major part of the evening thinking. I knew Beg was the mastermind in the area and if anyone was going to get hurt, it had to be his handy work. I decided I had to brief my key personal to be on the lookout for anything out of place, anything amiss.

"Even though we have enjoyed success in the area in the near past, we have to be careful. Retaliatory strikes by the militants cannot be ruled out. They may be required to do so to establish their lost control on the civil population. We have to be extra careful. Be on the lookout for changes in patterns, report if anything is out of place or amiss. Keep your guard up. We cannot take the situation lightly.", said I addressing my men.

"Please listen in on the radio networks. I want every transmission by Beg to be recorded and conveyed to me immediately.", I instructed the signal NCO. Post a little more of the discussions with my key appointments, I went back into deep thinking. When it got too much, I ordered my dinner and chose to watch a movie on television. It took an effort to shut up my mind and to lull myself to sleep. A soldier can sometimes be worried and more so for the safety of his own men. I could sense that there would be more strikes and such strikes could target my men, besides me.

"We have to get Beg at the earliest.", I knocked off to sleep with that thought. The coming days were going to be exciting enough.

The following morning I decided to have a chat with everyone I knew especially Ayaz and see if they knew anything about Beg. To my surprise, everyone denied having any knowledge of Beg. Not even Ayaz had heard of him. Ayaz recounted his days as a militant when he last had a radio set and denied the existence of anyone by that name. Now, of course, he did not have access to a radio set.

"Who are the prominent OGWs[21] in Magam?", I asked Ayaz.

"There are a few. Most are sympathisers only. Since, the battalion headquarters are located there, there is hardly any movement in Magam. Actually, OGWs of other neighbouring villages are more active. The OGWs in Magam are more for political reasons and for spreading their ideology. One cannot rule out their working as traffic cops once in a while to facilitate militant movement. But, militants rarely halt in Magam now.", said Ayaz.

"So, how do we find out about Beg?", I asked.

Ayaz too appeared clueless.

"I will try and find out. My hunch is that his real name is not Beg. That is what is going to make finding him difficult. I think I will start by finding who the most active OGWs in Magam are? So far, no one has been that interested in OGWs. I am sure Beg is not a militant going by your description.", said Ayaz.

For me, it was turning out to be more and more difficult to make a headway. In the meantime, Ayaz had come up with information of certain hideouts in the Bakiakar forest. I sensed there was always a possibility given that the G series spent a lot of their time there. A search of the area pond was carried out and a hideout found. The hideout was empty barring a few utensils. The hideout was destroyed and marked on the map.

---

[21] Overground Workers - a term used to represent those who actively engaged with and supported the militants.

I and Ayaz met on daily basis now or at least spoke over phone. Even Ayaz was unable to make any encouraging headway into the Beg case.

Meanwhile, Beg had been busy and becoming dangerous by the day.

Baisakhi - a Sikh festival was around the corner and I and my team were to travel to the neighbouring Sikh paltan (unit), where I was invited for the celebrations. The road to the destination went around the contiguous hills around Magam through some of the neighbouring company areas.

On the fateful day, I started out on a light vehicle - a Maruti Gypsy with a small team of 6 heading north east via village Kawari. I was running late and therefore, in a relative hurry for I did not wish to be late. Other senior officers of the sector were going to be there. I was well into the neighbouring company area by now preoccupied with this thought.

The sight was magnificent with open paddy fields to my right and left and a high mountain ridge running parallel to the road further on to my left. The Kashmir Valley is at its most beautiful in the month of April. With the onset of spring, one can spot hues of yellows, greens and all possible shades in the middle. Add to that the flowers on the trees and bushes and one gets a really beautiful picture. I was immersed in the pretty sight when the beautiful trance I was in, was broken by a loud bang from an explosion ahead of me. The loudness was ear shattering that jolted me into the present. I could not immediately see what had happened. About five hundred meters ahead, I could see a plume of black smoke indicating the plausible location of the explosion.

Since I could not hear of any ensuing gun fire, I decided to speed towards it. 50 meters short of the spot, I halted my vehicle. The team dismounted and leaving behind one person, the others quickly reached the spot. It was a gory sight. An IED had been activated that had caught another military vehicle - a Maruti gypsy and the occupants lay tattered and bloodied on the road. There were six in all of which three were alive but injured. I quickly called up my vehicle and dispatched those injured to the nearest medical aid post after a quick first aid. Those who weren't lucky enough to survive were moved next using other civil vehicles which had been difficult to find. I called in additional reinforcements to cover the area from the company responsible for the area. One of the martyrs was a senior officer from the neighbouring unit. The Baisakhi program had gone for a toss and all of a sudden, the valley didn't look so beautiful.

Once things had eased a little, I looked around and found the setting was quite similar to what had been created earlier in Batpura. Except this time, instead of a tractor trolley, a broken down Sumo had been used to slow the traffic down.

"Was this another trap for me actually?", I thought.

"They have gone really far this time. The IED was set up in a completely different area. How did they know?"

"Could it be that they got the other vehicle by mistake? After all, both the vehicles looked very similar."

Again there was no vegetation on either side of the road at the site affording good clear view of the area. The nearest habitation was 3 kilometres away and there was no traffic on the road. Someone must have tipped off providing an early warning and another sitting on the ridge would have activated the IED. Perhaps the IED handlers were so located that they could not see my vehicle approaching and activated the IED remotely when they found the first vehicle matching the description, approach the site. The engineers detachment on the site had confirmed a radio controlled IED had been detonated in this case.

9

Payback time!

I was feeling both angry and guilty at the same time. Guilty for innocent blokes had lost their lives and angry since I badly wanted to do something about it but was unable to make any headway.

I finally returned to base after a long day out - a day filled with remorse for the loss of lives earlier that day. I quietly vowed that I will not rest until I had taken revenge for the loss. I spent the entire night thinking. By the morning, I had a plan. I also had a theory. I figured out two primary things. Firstly, that whoever it was, was out to get me and he couldn't be acting alone. He needed a set of militants to carry out the attacks while he sat coordinating it all. There had to be lookouts keeping an eye on my movements and acting as tip offs.

Secondly, even if Beg was difficult to catch, the militants could be easier and they were most probably operating out of the high ridge forest that separated Batpura from Kawari - a high ground that afforded great visibility and was covered with a forest that facilitated easy, undetected cross movement. I decided that it could be easier to first tackle the militants and thus, destroy Beg's weapon while the search for Beg continued.

I figured that I had to be at two places at the same time - on the roads as a bait and in the jungle because I personally wanted to hunt down the militants. I was also not sure if Beg thought he had got his man earlier. The radio interceptions had indicated Beg's knowledge of the attack earlier that day but nowhere did he sound excited. Either, he knew I was missed or he was entirely cold in the heart. I had to let it be known that I was alive and kicking.

The next day, I undertook a long patrol in my area and covered nearly six villages talking to prominent people all along. I was sure the word would reach Beg one way or the other. I acted nonchalant and made an effort to appear calm. I kept up the routine for the next couple of days, even going all the way to Magam on one of my trips. I did not want Beg to pull down the apparatus created to get me.

That I had created enough noise to be noticed by everyone became clear soon. Beg was again appearing to be under pressure on the radio, the recent strike not withstanding.

I figured it was time to roll out the hunt.

I first took Haider into confidence and the agreed patch of the forest where I suspected the presence of militants was made out of bounds for any other team of security forces. I knew that though the militants could be living in the forest, they needed to depend on the villages nearby for their logistic requirements. The plan was therefore, simple - melt into the forest and systematically observe routes connecting fringe villages with the forest. The difficult part was remaining hidden in the forest undetected for such a long period of time. Additionally, I was required to be also present in public eye. I had to make a choice - to be the hunter or the bait. This time of course, the choice wasn't difficult to make for only I could be the bait. In the absence of the bait, the hunter would have been useless.

I now bid for another young officer to be the hunter. My choice was Rambo (of course his nickname) - a dynamic young officer who looked like a Kashmiri himself and could live off the land for long periods of time. A hugely motivated man who was forever willing to take on any militant. His was a very interesting story as well but maybe that could be the subject of another book. He was fearless and operated like a commando of which he was additionally proud. Only the fittest could keep up with him and so he had a small team too of equally fit people. Haider was able to spare Rambo for the operation who arrived with his small team of five at my op base. Haider too wanted revenge for the loss in the recent IED blast in the battalion area.

Rambo was equally charged and upbeat about the impending operation. The IED that had gone off was in the area where Rambo operated. He was therefore, raring to go.

Rambo and his team were to remain undercover and survive by themselves as long as they could in the jungle.

Rambo was to open his radio sets for communication twice daily. I had access to battery chargers while Rambo did not. So, I could keep my radio sets open all the time. I was to inform and coordinate Rambo's movement with mine. In case of an emergency, Rambo could always call in. Rambo's team was self contained for three days and every third day logistic replenishments were to reach Rambo's team. The plan was to persist with the operations for at least seven days. The weather in April was expected to hold out and it was not very cold at night. Furthermore, Rambo's team was to go under cover and hence, operate in clothes matching that of the locals.

I and Rambo got along pretty well and spent the evening enjoying ourselves and talking about all possible contingencies - codewords, places for a meet up, etc. The talking helped.

The following night at 2 AM a team of eighteen left the op base and moved towards Batpura on the road. Rambo's team of six in plain clothes and firans were offloaded enroute and they quickly climbed towards the forest. The remaining twelve remained in the area for another hour and came back to the base by first light. Rambo's team had successfully inserted into the area.

Rambo's team was to find a secluded place where they could set up base in the forest such that they would not be disturbed or spotted by any locals coming in. The forest itself was reached after climbing a rather steep and high mountain ridge. The height desisted the locals from climbing normally. Hence, not too much traffic was expected in any case. The plan for the first day was simple. Hide in the forest and observe the area. Establish movement patterns of locals if any. Additionally, they were to identify spots that could be used for surveillance from the next day.

Rambo's team was going to observe a strict routine whereby they were to eat before first light and after last light only. They were also required to conserve their energy and water. They could sleep leaving sentry guards at night. The day started early and ended late. The team was required to display extreme caution and discipline. More importantly, all six were required to be mentally alert at all times. The boys chosen were, therefore, such who relished the adventure and the challenge it posed. Rambo had to exercise extreme control on each member of his team to ensure no accidents. Thus, at all times, he had to know what each member of his team was doing.

The first day went in simply observing. There were no patterns yet - it was too early for that. Generally, the team was on the lookout for anyone coming into the forest who appeared to be carrying stuff for more than one's own personal requirement or in other cases people standing around for no clear reason - perhaps as look outs and all this had to be done from the fringes of the forest undetected. Rambo figured six men moving together anywhere is difficult to hide. Hence, only two moved along the fringes while four remained hidden slightly deeper into the forest but within earshot. The first day went in purely observing. It turned out to be a rather long day. Rambo was severely challenged through the day as he was not used to sleeping over unanswered questions. He found it difficult to control himself if he spotted any local and it took quite an effort to not catch the local and interrogate. I had especially warned Rambo against doing any such thing.

I knew that in case the cover was blown and the villagers learnt of Rambo's presence, they would definitely come and report. They may not report presence of real militants but that of Army men in guise was always reported. I was then compelled to reward for the information but everyone knew it is not going to hurt anyone and hence, no one was under threat. Thankfully, nothing of the kind happened.

On day two, Rambo's team decided to monitor the slopes towards village Batpura. The lack of vegetation on the slopes helped the cause. Rambo soon realised that the presence of road opening teams by day along the road and the lack of vegetation made it virtually impossible for anyone to carry out any suspicious activity this side of the forest patch. If anything at all was possible, it could happen either before the road opening team gets in place or after they leave. Accordingly, Rambo was in location well before first light at 5 AM. The days were getting longer. This was going to be another long one.

Rambo had chosen an ideal spot. It was a kink in the slopes jutting out from the top like someone's forehead. The area was well vegetated and the nature of the feature posed a steep climb onto it. It was away from any tracks leading up and was therefore avoided by the locals. The outstretched nature allowed for extended visibility of the slopes though. It was a rather boring task. To sit or rather lie down idle, under cover and observe the area was challenging for someone who loved action and being on the move. Add to that, the added challenge of keeping quiet and the degree of difficulty multiplies. And now to do that for more than 12 hours at a stretch can test anyone. Surveillance is an art not everyone can master.

Major part of the day was uneventful. Very few climbed into the forest or left it through the day. Most who did were the one's taking their live stock and that of the village for grazing on the slopes or in the forest. No-one seemed to move suspiciously - a few kids who chased each other on the hill slopes, a few isolated bakarwals, an occasional lady in search of firewood. The entire day's monotony was broken only by the mid day snack. Today the 'shakarparas' tasted rather sweet. These were my favourite too. A chocolate was the star attraction. A fauji can draw pleasure out of simple things that are otherwise taken for granted.

The end of the day was rather challenging. As soon as the road opening party lifted, frantic activity started on the forest slopes. Today a wood smuggler had planned to sneak out wood. He and his accomplices were busy at work. Some ladies were returning with firewood. Nothing notable had happened through the day. It was suddenly pitch dark. And perhaps the right time for the team to upstick. Rambo's team was rather hungry now. They had to get to their chosen hideout in the forest for the night. Quickly get their dinner ready and catch whatever little sleep they could before the next day's routine started. Thankfully, pre-cooked rations came in handy. A meal of steamed rice and dal makhni was prepared in twenty minutes, consumed in the next ten and the team settled down for the night. It was already 9 PM and they had to be ready for the next day's schedule by 4 AM after consuming breakfast at an unearthly hour.

Soldiers often bear such hardships. After all, all the training at the academies was to build this endurance. If the leader could endure, the men will follow his example. Rambo decided to take the first turn at keeping watch with his buddy. The night in the forests in Kashmir can be really quiet. The low temperatures and the altitude ensure there are no insects around. Lack of insects keeps reptiles away as also the noise they make. The quiet can be extremely strenuous. Sometimes, in the quiet, one can start to imagine sounds where there are none especially when one is stressing hard to hear with the only sensory organs that can help in the pitch dark. That night it was so quiet that one could hear one's heartbeat.

Barring one incident of cackling of some birds in the forest, the night had gone off peacefully. The reason for the birds getting disturbed could not be ascertained. But human intervention looked improbable. It could be some predator though.

Ready early the next morning, the team headed back to the same point for surveillance. They had to get in before it was daylight.

In the meantime, I was busy keeping up with my visits to the villages and meeting as many people as I could. The conversations with Rambo had not yielded any encouraging indicators yet. Things looked perfectly in order. If any militants were operating out of the forest, there were no signs of it yet. I, however, decided to stick to the original plan at the least for the seven days we had decided originally. I chose to undertake a vehicle based patrol towards Batpura simply to observe if anything changes. Nothing did. Things were as normal as the previous days. There were no perceptible tell tale signs at all. It was getting rather frustrating for me. There had been two attacks from the area and there were no signs now, whatsoever.

The following day too went past quietly with nothing much to take note of. I had planned to link up with and meet Rambo in the evening. It had been three days since Rambo's team had been living on self contained rations. On the third day, in the evening, a vehicle check post was set up at the junction of the Batpura-Kawari road. The plan was simple. Half of my team will continue to check people on the road and keep the area sanitised, while the remaining half would climb up into the forest at night fall and link up with Rambo's team. Things moved as per plan and a little around 8.30 PM, Rambo and I sat chatting up. Rambo's team was happy enjoying a full cooked fresh meal after three days. Fresh supplies and change of clothing was handed over, whereas used material was collected from Rambo's team.

"There are absolutely no tell tale signs of any militant presence this side, even though, I would have liked to interrogate a few people personally.", said Rambo.

"So, what do you think, should we do?", I asked.

"I am not sure.", said Rambo enjoying the chicken curry I had brought along for him.

"I think let us stick to the plan. It is by and large clear that this side of the forest slopes are clear. But we still have to sanitise the other side.", I continued, referring to the Kawari side of the forest. "Let us shift our focus to the other side starting tomorrow."

"Alright sir!", acknowledged Rambo.

"You do understand that communication with base that side will be tough at times now. You may chose to relay messages through your company that will be more accessible communication wise.", I said.

"I understand sir. That side I am much more familiar with. After all, that is my area.", said Rambo excitedly.

Well! Alright then! I think we should be going. Wishing you luck. Please be careful. Do not take unnecessary risks. It's also easy to get fatigued now!", I said.

"My team is raring for action sir! I hope we get it soon.", with that Rambo saluted me and was gone. His team merged into the forest darkness.

My team was going to hang around a little longer before starting the descent. The area needed to be cleared as well. I did not wish to leave behind a trail of trash either. By

9 PM, my team had begun the descent and linked up with the other half.

The following morning, Rambo's team started early and in high spirits. It's surprising what a fresh meal and some good conversation can do to a soldier. Rambo needed the motivation of the previous evening. The team had now shifted focus to the opposite side of the forest overlooking the areas where the IED had gone off. Rambo had first decided to oversee the slopes leading into villages Kawari and Jagarpora.

I had decided to stay away from the area for the day lest increased interest in the area be noticed by the people. I instead spent the time meeting as many people as possible including those who passed by the base. With a keen eye on the lookout for any signs, I could have learnt a lot by casually talking to passers by. Rambo's team appeared to be doing a good job of hiding their identity. It would have been otherwise easy to be picked up by the locals. However, the evening conversation was nothing encouraging. Again there appeared to be no signs whatsoever. Rambo, however, enjoyed learning so much more about his area. The following day, Rambo was to continue the surveillance and I had decided to take the road towards Kawari on foot.

The following morning came. It was a Sunday. The Road Opening Team had a rare day off. Rambo's team was already in place, having gone a little farther than the previous day. I chose to move out with my team in the direction of village Kawari. The roads were mostly deserted with little to no vehicular movement. People were busy having a quiet Sunday morning. I was once again busy with my thought process.

"The roads are very quiet this morning."

"What if we get no result in the forest? This will turn out to be an exercise in futility."

"What if Rambo has a contact with the militants? They are only six and any help will take a long time to reach them."

Lost in my thoughts, I did not even realise that the team had taken the turn towards village Kawari. The team had gone barely 200 meters from the turn that we came under fire. It is then that I realised that we had reached a point on the road that was hugging the mountain slope onto one side and the river on to the other. The first half of the team had barely come in the open when the fire started. The team was trained to immediately seek cover. Someone found a tree, another the slight embankment on the road. A small cutting in the slope on the roadside seemed to afford the best cover. One of the boys was hurt with a bullet scraping one of his arms. He was bleeding but in full senses. I quickly took stock of the situation. Everyone was under cover. A few militants were perched on the slope above and were firing pinning down my team. It was a big surprise for me. Militants were on the back foot and not known to expose themselves in such a manner. But they had chosen their site well. Perhaps they no longer wanted to depend on an IED or they were out of explosives.

For my team to move out of cover would have been suicidal. The road was well exposed and with the river on the other side, there was no where to go. The mountain slope itself was too steep and exposed by the day to make an assault uphill. The militants seemed to be firing from a position hidden within a few trees on the slope. The location was onto a limb and farthest away from any of the op bases. The militants had surprised me. I continued to encourage my men to stay in cover and intermittently returned fire towards the possible militant location.

My team was pinned down and the militants were shouting profanities and challenging me to come out of cover and show up. I knew better. I figured I needed to keep my machismo in check. I was also thankful that the militants had finally shown up.

"My hunch was right!"

I was pinned down but I was also the bait. So, 'no problem'. I continued to keep control on my team. I only had one simple objective now. I had to keep the militants in location. I was only hoping that Rambo would have heard the firing. He was after all not more than 2 kilometres from the spot as the crow flies. And yet again, I was proven right.

"Rambo for Maqbool!", came the transmission on radio. It was Rambo and he could be heard gasping for breath in between the call. Sure enough, he was moving fast.

"Rambo! The prey has finally shown up and bitten the bait. They are on the slope towards Kawari on Gosain Teng top 300-400 meters above the road. We are trying to keep them held up in location. You know what you have to do!", I replied.

"Roger!", came the crisp reply.

I knew we only had to keep the militants in place a little longer. The militants would have anticipated the fastest counter reaction would come using the roads over which they had visibility for kilometres. I knew calling in reinforcements by road would give the militants the signal to scoot. I, of course, did not want that. It was now a matter of ten minutes on the outside by which Rambo would be effective, much sooner than the militants would have anticipated anyone coming to my rescue.

I now urged my team to ensure that the militants are not allowed to run away. The excitement buoyed by the adrenaline rush was palpable. I was trying hard to hold myself back. But I could not afford to come out of cover. The site worked well for the militants in pinning down my team but they had only one route to escape and that was backwards and upslope. They were of course in no hurry to escape yet especially when the job for them was not done yet. They thought, they had their prey pinned down. For me, every minute felt like an hour. Not everyone in my team knew what was happening with reinforcements. The natural instinct of a trained soldier was to fight back - a few even willing to sacrifice themselves for their buddies. I obviously couldn't shout and tell them just yet but had to ensure they remained under cover and protected. I had regained my composure and was calm under fire now - the only sure shot way of conveying to my team that I knew what I was doing and therefore, get them to follow my command.

"Stay under cover! Just another 10 minutes to go!", I shouted.

"Come out you cowards!", shouted the militants. "I am going to kill you!", challenged a militant.

"Stay calm!", I shouted to my men ignoring the militant.

And then the friendly fire started. Rambo's team reached the top from the other side. They were in location now to bring fire down upon the militants who were hiding in a small clump of trees on the slope. Least expecting this, the militants were in disarray - not knowing what to do.

I directed my team to take position and shoot down anyone who tries to run. Only one did and was dealt with. He thought he could run downhill fast and maybe escape bullets. Only his dead body reached the base having been shot midway. The firefight was suddenly over. It was once again quiet now. One could hear the shots echoing far away in the valley. I needed to take things in control.

I called in a vehicle each from my op base and the battalion headquarters. The boy who was hurt in the arm was given first aid. Thankfully, it was not so serious. His bone had been spared. No one else was hurt which was a miracle. One of the dead militants lay on the road next to my team. The others still needed to be physically flushed out from their hiding.

Rambo's team lay in position. I had asked them to not move till I reached, after which the mopping up of the area was to start.

Leaving half of my team below, I took a circuitous route to the clump of trees. This allowed both the other teams to be able to fire if needed while they could see my half team approaching the target. My team fired at the target while a little short of it. There was no return of fire. We finally reached the objective to find three more dead terrorists. It was somewhat clear that they had arrived and occupied the ambush site in a hurry since they had not been able to booby trap the killing ground where they had planned to trap my team. Also the site as seen from the terrorists' location was not so clearly open. Perhaps they had thought that they could fell me with the opening burst of their weapons. Luckily, that had not happened and they continued being in the location a little too long out of frustration or over confidence. They clearly had no idea of Rambo's team's presence in the forest above, else they would have made a getaway sooner. I was particularly happy to have survived to fight another day yet again. I knew hunts don't turn out particularly well for the bait.

The four dead bodies had been recovered from the site. Haider too had fetched up along with the vehicles from the headquarters. He was happy on the success of the operation and congratulated both Rambo and me. I had decided to, for once, celebrate being alive with Rambo the same evening.

I knew now that Beg's weapon for now had been neutralised but Beg was still at large. Beg could get more weapons and therefore, it was important to neutralise Beg at the earliest. Beg had relayed the bad news to his bosses across the same evening. Four newly recruited HM militants had been killed that day. They had come in to avenge the loss to their tanzeem at my hand. My area was an important transit area for the militants and therefore, they were desperate to take things under control. Barring the successful IED attack the previous week, nothing much was going their way. While I and Rambo enjoyed the evening celebrating the success of the operation with the team, I now had Beg all over my mind.

"I can see you are not entirely here, sir!", suggested Rambo to me.

"Yes! My mind is on the handlers. You know of course, what has been going on. I need to get to Beg earliest. He is the mastermind. We have hunted down four today, another four may surface anytime. But to put some end to this problem, I have to figure out and neutralise Beg.", I said.

"I understand sir! I will also put in some energy towards finding out who Beg is.", said Rambo. "I am thankful to you for choosing me for this operation. It feels great to taste success."

"Rambo! You deserve the credit for this operation. You and your team executed beautifully. Had that not been the case, the rats wouldn't have come out of the hole. Cheers to that!", I said, sensing it was not the time to spoil the moment.

"Cheers sir!"

That night Rambo and I sat till late with our teams recollecting the details of the operation and rejoicing our success. It helped bust stress.

I, however, could not entirely relax. I had to figure out Beg's real identity and nab him at the earliest. However, so far, it appeared that only a divine intervention could make it happen for there was absolutely no clue as to who Beg was. My sources of information were proving ineffective. It was clear that Beg was a name for the radio only. In real life, Beg was someone else. But he exercised great trust amongst the militant tanzeems.

10

An unlikely brush with Beg!

The following morning, I saw off Rambo who was returning to his base. Soon after, I remembered that Ayaz had been trying to contact me and he was talking about some militants operating out of village Kawari.

Kawari was the farthest village under my responsibility and the approach took one through the same spot where the recent fire fight had happened. It was flanked by the forested mountain tops on to one side with the river on the other. There was a bridge over the river right at the end of the village. On crossing the bridge, one crossed the national highway connecting Kupwara with Handwara and Sopore. Immediately next, one could climb onto a ridge line that connected areas of the dreaded Lolab valley to the north and Sopore to the south. I always thought that the Kawari bridge was a very important crossing point. But it was impossible to cover the bridge undetected.

I got in touch with Ayaz who was over in no time. Ayaz seemed to have no idea of what happened two days earlier in the ambush by the militants. I wanted to know if it could be the same set of militants that he had information on. Ayaz denied.

"The information I had was about a militant who has been crossing over from the other side quite regularly and visiting the lambardar's house in the village.", said Ayaz.

"As I understand, on the other side of the river, there is no place to stay by, no village. Are they operating from the forest the rest of the time? I can understand crossing over but not prolonged operations.", I said thinking out loud. "To me initially, it seems I cannot do much.", I spoke the last bit very softly such that only I could hear.

For me though, Beg still was top of my mind. I had decided to go after Beg hammer and tongs. The more I thought about figuring out Beg, the more the problem in Kawari looked addressable to me. Thinking hard, I realised that for me launching an operation in village Kawari was much easier to think through than find a way to nab Beg. After all, I was a soldier and trained to be one. Beg was a completely different kind of challenge.

"Let me figure out Kawari tomorrow and see what can be done.", I thought to myself.

The following morning I set out for Kawari. The village was really far from the op base and the bridge even farther away. On the way, lay the ambush site which I was particularly careful in crossing this time. I had to walk through the village to get to the other side where the bridge lay. Close to the bridge, there was just one solitary house. The village had grown till a little short of the bridge and the lone house lay just beyond the bridge. From there onwards, it was a walk in the clear for a kilometre until just short of where one could cross the Kupwara-Sopore road. An upslope rose on to the other side immediately beyond, that connected with the ridge line beyond.

On the way back, I stopped on the bridge to look around. It was in the open and afforded visibility over a long distance on all sides. The river flowing below the bridge formed the Eastern boundary of my area of responsibility and ran all the way till a little short of Handwara where it turned eastwards but only after another stream joined the river. This other stream formed the southern boundary. A kilometre beyond the village Kawari, another smaller stream joined the river that flowed parallel and next to the line of villages of which Batpura was a part. The solitary house near the bridge made very little sense. I guessed that perhaps this house played a vital role in the crossings whenever those took place.

As I re-entered the village from the bridge side, I decided to visit the lambardar. It was quite customary to do so and perceived nothing out of the ordinary.

The lambardar's house was a double storied house in the middle of the village built on a high plinth. The house had a high boundary marked with roofing sheets on three sides. I stood at the gate and called out for those at home. It took a good five minutes for anyone to come out. When someone did, it was a young girl who informed that the lambardar was not at home. I decided to turn away and continue to the op base. I had barely gone 100 meters when the lambardar came running behind to meet me. I had a casual chat asking about his well being and continued on the way to the op base. On the way, it did occur to me that the entire episode was a little odd. If the lambardar was away, how did he suddenly appear a little later. The statements given by his daughter and that of the lambardar were also not entirely coherent. The same evening a radio interception suggested that indeed there could have been a few militants in the lambardar's house when I had reached there casually. One militant 'Yakoob' was busy narrating how they had a narrow escape while the Army landed up at the very house they were holed up in. Without giving out any names of the village or the house owner, the militant was glad to have gotten away, their confidence in the house owner's loyalty towards them rising after the initial doubts.

I figured that Ayaz's report could be correct after all and also wondered how was it that Ayaz always knew, that too about areas as far away as the village Kawari. But then, I had better things to think about. Like whether to address the problem in Kawari or not? And if yes, then how to make it happen? Perhaps the answer to the first question lay in that of the second. As of now, the answer to the second question was not crystallising itself. Just when I was thinking that I would have to airdrop a team at the bridge for them to arrive undetected, it occurred to me that it was indeed possible to trap the militants as the village especially the bridge was visible from the hill top - Gosain Teng. The very hill from where I had been ambushed a few days before.

"I need not station a team in there or at the bridge.', I thought. "We should just observe using Night Vision Devices (NVD) and move in when we know the militants are crossing the bridge." Of course, the operation needed much more planning and observation. I then decided, I had to first do what Rambo had done. Spend a night atop Gosain Teng and simply observe.

I and my team of six - the same team that had missed the G series in Bakiakar, now inserted via the battalion headquarters at Magam. The ridge line connected with Gosain Teng and I planned to take a long circuitous walk along the ridge line to Gosain Teng and be in position to observe Kawari. Unfortunately, the insertion had to be done every night. The Thermal Imager(TI) sight that provided the requisite observation range at night ran on batteries that needed charging everyday. Two batteries supported the operation with intermittent switching on and off of the sight. I had only two batteries. Rambo and Haider both knew about what I had planned this time. Rambo was additionally ready to react fastest if needed, being the closest. Rambo had a Mine Protected Vehicle (MPV) at his disposal and was more than eager to put it to use. He could reach Kawari in less than 20 minutes if required.

My team was making good distance in the evening twilight through the forest. We were walking as fast as we could just below the ridge. There was very little underbrush along the ridge and in less than an hour, we were atop

Gosain Teng. The team quickly deployed itself in position to observe Kawari. Tale - the talented scout was to handle the thermal imager while I sat next to him. Rest of the team had deployed itself behind me facing backwards. It was going to be a long night, I hoped for it to be at least interesting.

The view from the mountain top was truly breathtaking. One could see for miles along the valley floor. In the distance, Kupwara town was visible with its lights lit. Nearer and to the south lay Handwara. Numerous other clusters of lights indicated a host of villages on the valley floor. In my own area, all movement had seized after 8 PM except at the fringes where it was difficult for the Army teams to patrol. People liked to sleep early, and it was a sight to see house after house switch off their lights as they settled in to go to sleep. Slowly, entire villages went off to sleep while the team of soldiers kept awake, on the lookout. This is also when the dogs took over as if the night belonged to them. Surprisingly, I realised for the first time in nearly two years that Kawari did not have a single dog. While dogs came alive in the rest of the villages every now and then, Kawari remained silent through the night. Barring one or two tube lights in the village, the village was largely dark which worked well for the thermal imagers. Now the wait began. The target for observation were the bridge and the lambardar's house.

Until about 9 PM, traffic plied on the Handwara - Kupwara round and every once in a while someone, returning perhaps from another city, would alight on the road and then be seen scuttling towards Kawari via the bridge. Such movement was quite easily perceived and relatable since the vehicles plying on the road could be identified with their headlights. Post 9 PM though, it was all very quiet. Vehicular traffic had now subsided. The darkness slowly enveloped everything. The height where the team was perched gave one a bird's eye view. I calculated that for anyone to come down from the opposite ridge line and then walk across to the lambardar's house would require approximately 30 minutes of walking time. Hence, it was decided that the TI sight be switched on every half an hour and the area be scanned for any movement.

The movement I was really interested in happened soon afterwards. A little past 10 PM, two people walked into the village over the bridge. This was no ordinary movement as the two people stopped a couple of times as if to ascertain if things were alright. It appeared as if someone signalled to them and only after that they crossed the bridge into the village. It was difficult to figure out who the signaller was. The two walked into the middle of the village close to where the lambardar's house was and then could be traced no more. Clearly, they did not use the main lane leading upto the lambardar's house else they would have been spotted. Now the long wait started again. It was crucial to pick up when they left. The entire night went in figuring out just that. It was only at 3.15 AM in the morning that any movement happened again. Two personal again emerged from inside the village and disappeared down the track towards the ridge on the opposite side. It was difficult to say if these were the same two people but the movement was suspicious enough. With very little of the second battery left, it was also time for the team to move back to the op base before the villages woke up and spotted my team's movement.

I decided that we will strike the night after next. I figured it would be better if my team rested for a while before that. I spent the day preparing for the operation with my team, fine tuning the various contingencies, figuring out how things could pan out differently from planned.

The following day, I left with my team - a total of eight this time, for the battalion headquarters where we rested for half the day. Close to dusk, the team started the climb up to Magam top and then proceeded briskly towards Gosain Teng occupying the very same spot as we had done two nights before. This time, I and my scout Tale were in direct communication. Tale was on the TI sight. I would have loved to take him along further but I needed an expert on the sight. I and three of my best i.e. half the team now descended half the way down into position and in cover. With radio communication checked, the team worked to regain normal breathing. It was already 9 PM. I knew I could not descend into the village yet.

Now the wait started.

Yet again, in wait, the world around went to sleep. The valley floor was getting dark, the heights were surprisingly starlit. The frequency of traffic slowed down and then died. It feels strange when everything around is slowly stopping over while one is busy at work. The sight though produced a feeling of stillness and was therefore calming. The lights of Kupwara and Handwara towns were visible in the far distance and dimmed rapidly affecting the ambient light in the valley. Today, the valley was pitch dark, however, the upper layers were lit with ambient light that slowly darkened. And while it became pitch dark, I wondered what must be going on for it was nearly 10 PM. I decided to call Tale.

"Maqbool for Tale!"

"Tale for Maqbool!", replied Tale.

"Any movement seen?",

"Nako Hajoor!", replied Tale in the negative in Nepali.

I would be very disappointed if the militants did not show up. The wait became only longer. I was looking at my watch fervently and ever so often. It was only 10.45 PM. Tale still had nothing to report. I was now getting fidgety. I was so sure that I would get my prey that I had just not figured what to do if the militants did not show up. I had no options but to wait. Time, however, was passing rather slowly. With no TI sight, I had nothing much to do except wait. I knew my eyes were up there with Tale and we could only succeed by trusting each other. My half team was carrying Infra Red (IR) based night vision devices but those had short battery lives and even shorter range. The wait was well and truly on. Touching base with Tale every half an hour, I only received news in the negative. Finally, around 2 AM, I was faced with the decision making dilemma of what to do.

"Should I move back and come another day?"

"We would have to get moving by 3.30 AM at the latest to avoid detection.", I thought. But then a thought struck me.

"Maqbool for Tale!"

"Tale for Maqbool, over!", came the reply.

"I want you to observe the house and not the bridge now.", I said.

"Roger sir!", Tale confirmed.

Very soon, Tale responded.

"Tale for Maqbool, the lambardar's home is mostly dark but for one room where lights came on briefly and I could sense some movement inside. The lights are off again and came on at least twice in between.", reported Tale.

I got thinking. I suspected that the militants may have stayed over from the previous day. Now came the dilemma yet again.

"Should I move in - if they are there and if they try to move out, we could engage them successfully. However, if they are not there, we could be detected and never get another chance.", I thought. "But if they are not there, then why the movement in lambardar's house at this hour? This means that they are there and could be preparing to leave. We must move in."

With my mind made, I signalled my team of four to move forward.

"Maqbool for Tale! We are moving in! Be on the lookout. Also inform base."

"Roger sir!", replied Tale.

For the operation today, an additional battery for the TI sight had been carried along from the battalion headquarters. Tale quickly passed on the message to both the base and Rambo's operator that my team was inserting for the operation and got back to observing the lambardar's house and my half team alternately. Keeping an eye on the house was more important though.

My half team descended from our location and entered the village. I had chosen jungle boots for the operation over the more versatile DMS boots used otherwise. The shoes had rubber soles that were relatively quieter. The team inserted into the village like ghosts. The road leading to the bridge passed from behind the lambardar's house. However, onto the other side of the road, there were no houses as the steep embankment lowered rapidly towards the river. This is where the team quickly got into position - the two buddy pairs approximately 10 meters apart. On either side of the house, narrow lanes passed connecting with the road. None of the windows of the target house opened on to the road side. This worked well for my team while the team moved into position but not so well after the team got into position for it offered no observation of what was happening inside the house. The house opened onto the lane and the only way of now spotting any activity was to keep an eye on the gate leading on to the narrow lanes. A quick contact with Tale confirmed that the target had not left the house as yet. It was already 3 AM. I knew there wasn't much time left to wait for. At most, the wait would be over in an hour or the operation will have to be called off. The final outcome depended on whether my team had managed to avoid detection. Once again the wait started. It's surprising how a very large part of the soldier's job was playing the waiting game and to keep one's nerves under control while at it.

The wait did not last very long though. I was personally positioned to cover any movement down the lane that lead to the main gate of lambardar's house. In about 20 minutes after the team got into position, I could hear some sound coming from the target house but no movement was visible. Then, I could next hear distinct metal sound as would emanate when someone moved large metal sheets. But again nothing was visible. I called Tale but Tale could not pick up any movement either. I now switched on my own IR goggles to scan the area for any movement. The metallic sound had ceased but no one was visible. I called for Tale and asked him to scan the area. Almost simultaneously, both I and Tale spotted two militants appear onto the road a little further down the road than anticipated. Perhaps there was another way into the house which explained why we could not spot the militants entering the lambardar's house even the previous time.

I was now again faced with a split second dilemma of engaging or coming back another time. However, the miss at Bakiakar still haunted me. I did not want to miss the opportunity. I barely had a fraction of a second to make up my mind. I figured that no houses lay beyond the target in the line of fire and hence, opening fire was not risky at all. I directed my AK-47 towards the target and opened fire which was also the signal for my team to do so. And they were more than ready.

In a short but crisp burst of fire, the two militants fell on the road. They were dead for sure but the team received returning fire. It was a burst fired from the lane on the other side of the house.

"There were more of them!"

I and my team ducked to take evasive action and then returned the fire. But this time, there was no returning fire. I directed everyone to stop firing. It was my job to also figure that the figures firing at us had scooted from the scene. But Tale could see them. There were five more and they were now running towards the third side - not towards the bridge, not towards Gosain Teng but along the road towards the place where my team had been ambushed by the militants the previous month.

I figured the two militants frequenting the village were here to receive the others and were there to guide them elsewhere. Perhaps the other five came from the direction they were running backwards towards. I asked Tale if they could quickly descend from the hill top and engage the fleeing militants from the other side of the hill. I felt they would run towards Batpura. In the meantime, Rambo and his team had started from their base in a Mine Protected Vehicle (MPV) for village Kawari. I knew my other team from the op base will have started as well.

Leaving the other buddy pair to cover the two dead militants, I and my buddy decided to follow the fleeing militants. I knew it will all be over in less than twenty minutes.

I called Rambo and asked him to halt in Kawari and cover the lambardar's house until I returned. I knew that the five militants making a run could turn back only if an engagement with my other half team takes place. I also knew that no one in the village would step out having heard the bullets fired.

Having come out of the shadow of Gosain Teng, I was now in communication with my second team coming in from the op base and quickly briefed them on the situation. The team was briefed to move in and occupy positions covering the road connecting with the foot bridge next to Khanpura.

I had barely finished communicating with the other team leader when fire opened up yet again. This time the fire could be heard coming from the slopes of Gosain Teng and lasted for barely five minutes. I and my buddy quickly took up a position on the road side to cover any movement along the road as soon as the fire had started.

When firing stopped, Tale reported, "We reached just in time, the first man had just about crossed and ran away when we started firing. He did not even fire back. We got the next two and the last two ran backwards."

He had just finished speaking when those two running backwards reached my position. I and my buddy opened fire, engaged and felled the first militant. The second militant opened fire and ran towards Khanpura through the trees. He too was gunned down trying to cross the foot bridge by the reserve team that had managed to get in position just in time. In about 45 minutes, the fire fight had finally completely ceased and it was quiet again.

Everyone seemed to be catching up on their breath. I too was busy calming down the adrenaline that had kicked in. Visibility had slowly begun to improve as the new day began to break. For my team of course, it was time to start winding up the operation and seek some rest. But first, it was time to take stock. Rambo's team had reached Kawari and connected with the buddy pair left behind. He had things in control. Tale reported all was well. The reserve team too was perfectly alright and happy to have got a share of the action. I and my buddy were fine too.

Once again, Haider was on his way to the action site. I was happy for that. I knew with Haider around, I could hope for things to be wound up sooner. I and my team needed the break. I was tired and wanted to detach from the scene soonest. Rambo had already commenced the process of lifting the two dead militant bodies from the village. I wanted to interrogate the lambardar who had been summoned to the op base for a meet up later in the evening.

I wondered who was the lone figure who got away and why did he not fire.

"Did he not have a weapon on person?"

"Was he the guide?"

"Who could he be?"

Anyway, I was too fatigued to think about it further. I wanted to get some rest. Haider was happy for a very successful operation. I did not want to share all the details with Haider knowing that Haider would not have approved of some of my actions such as inserting into a village with just a four member team or then leaving just two behind and going after the fleeing militants in just a buddy pair. Something could have easily gone wrong. But I knew, I had taken a calculated risk and luckily things had worked in my favour.

I was happy, for getting six militants in an operation was big and that too without any casualty to own troops. I knew we had been extremely lucky. By 10 AM, I and my teams had returned to the op base. Everyone was in an upbeat mood. Tale especially, as he confided in me, "Saheb! I was thinking we will not get a share of the fun today. I am glad things turned out as they did."

"Never take things for granted, Tale!", I replied.

I realised that the operation was also a success because of the wonderful understanding the team members enjoyed between ourselves. An understanding that had developed through months of training and operating together. It was time to celebrate this understanding. My plan of always drawing a team out of a fixed pool of manpower that did not largely change over all these months except when someone was posted out or into the unit on completion of a tenure was paying rich dividends.

"We must celebrate!", and I decided to have a 'barakhana' organised for the company. The boys were upbeat and high on josh. They believed they could do anything successfully. Success can do that to you. Rambo too was invited to the 'barakhana' with his team. Rambo though was a tad unhappy for not being able to get a chance to fire his weapon this time. I pacified him with a few shots of fine whiskey that he enjoyed.

"I am sure you will get many more chances in the future. Let's enjoy the moment and celebrate!", I said to Rambo. Rambo stayed put with me that night.

Next morning, we were due to visit the battalion headquarters. Some documents and equipment were found on the dead militants and I wanted to take a look. The next day was packed but I decided to enjoy the moment as well. I was happy to see an otherwise very calm Tale, narrate how the operation unfolded animatedly to everyone present including Rambo. After all, he had a bird's eye view of the operation for most part. He was high on a few drinks and was enjoying himself. His facts though were absolutely in place.

In sensitive areas such as where my op base was, parties could not go on till late in the night. One could not afford to let one's guard down. So, the party was wound up by 10 PM and everyone retired much to the protests of Tale. Tale had to be suitably calmed down and put to sleep in his bed. He was not to be disturbed for the night.

I had by now been in enough operations to not let any post traumatic stress build up. I had perfected the art of switching off and delinking from any stresses of the previous days. That is the only way it worked for me.

Before sleeping, I decided to call Ayaz to let him know of the success. But his phone was switched off.

"Perhaps even Ayaz was celebrating our success."

There was always another day to call. With that, I decided to call that very eventful day a day and dozed off to sleep. The night after a hardworking success is a night filled with sweet dreams. I had hardly lied down that I was already in deep sleep.

The next morning came and the lambardar arrived at the op base to meet me as summoned. He looked apologetic and barely made any eye contact with me.

"Sir! I don't know where they came from?", was the standard reply. Of course, he had no idea that I knew they had been visiting for a while.

"They had guns and we were not allowed to move out of the house." I knew that too. "Even our phones were taken away."

"Perhaps!", I thought.

I allowed the lambardar to continue with his defensive rants. "My family's life is under threat."

That could be right after the encounter for his family would have been within the circle of suspicion by the militants. While he was busy weaving a story around the episode, I suddenly asked.

"Who was the person guiding them?" I knew he would definitely accept that, given that he may want his own life off the hook.

"There was someone from the local area itself. But he did not reveal much about himself.", said the lambardar.

"Can you describe him?"

"He was of medium height and spoke fluent Kashmiri and Urdu. He had arrived at night with some militants. In the dark, I could not even see his face clearly."

I knew that he could be lying and given what I knew about him, he was not likely to tell the truth. Anyway, I had to put caution into him.

"Lambardar Saheb! I am aware of what goes on in your village and for how long those two had been visiting and sometimes staying over at your place including on the day we met in your village. So, don't give me misleading stories. I need to know who it was. What is his name?", I asked sternly.

The lambardar was quiet now for a while. But sensing that I was not going to take any nonsense, he finally spoke, "I really don't know him. Someone nominates these people to act as guides. They do it for money. These guides then lead militant groups from one point to another. I assure you I did not have a choice. Typically, one can be punished for not helping and the punishment for betrayal is sure shot death. It is, therefore, better to accept the incentive of letting them pass through and be in their good books rather than confront them."

"Why are you chosen over others? You can chose to have nothing to do with them like many others?", I asked.

"Yes Saheb! That is right! But we are black mailed into it. My nephew had crossed over nearly six years back. We haven't heard from him ever since. It is with an anticipation of learning something about him that we let them come. We are also worried that he may be harmed if we do anything otherwise."

"Do you realise that what you are doing is even more dangerous? In the hope of recovering your one family member, you are risking the lives of everyone else in the family.", I said. "I also do not see the logic in your story. If your nephew is across, you should be receiving sympathy. I see that as no reason to harbour militants. I am inclined to hand you over to the police formally but I will give you time to improve first. If I hear another instance of you harbouring militants, I will not spare you. If for some reason you have to, you must inform me, at least after they leave. Is that understood by you?", I concluded with a finality to it.

"Ji Saheb!", the lambardar could not have responded any other way. Whether he complies or not, only time was to tell. I knew the compulsion went beyond just the nephew story. He must enjoy the power and the economic benefit the support brought his way. In the absence of any incriminating evidence, I knew the lambardar will never see any serious repercussions come his way. I hoped that his reporting even after the militants leave will be of some value. I signalled for the lambardar to be removed from the op base and be allowed to leave. In a way, it worked in my favour to let him operate. At least I knew where to focus in Kawari.

It was now time to leave for Magam. I planned to have a word with Ayaz over phone when I got there. Even though I knew that Ayaz would somehow already know.

The radio intercepts of the previous day had confirmed the identity of the militants killed. They were all mercenaries from across. I wondered what made them come across.

"Is it religious ideology or the search for a meaning in life that they come across to lead a very risky life?", I thought. "Whatever be the reason, our job was to unite them with their maker."

11

The Beg mystery!

On reaching Magam, I went in to meet Haider who was happy with the outcome of the operation. He had been waiting to hear of the details and was surprised to hear of many of them. I shared the part how one person had gotten away and was apparently unarmed. He was in the lead and clearly got away that night.

"I was wondering if it was Beg. And if it was him, I am going to be haunted by the thought of him getting away even more.", I said to Haider. "No one would want him as badly as I do."

"I can understand that!", said Haider.

"All I need is a small help - a clue and I will do everything possible to get him."

"Well! Yes! I guess this man is very smart and covers himself phenomenally well. As of now, we are really dependent on some lucky break. One thing is sure that with the series of reversals that militant groups have received at your hand, Beg is under tremendous pressure.

We can expect him to make some mistakes. And that mistake should give up his identity.", said Haider. "Now let us go and enjoy the afternoon. We need to celebrate our success."

"What about the stuff found on the militants?"

"Yes! I have called for it to the mess. We can see things there over a glass of beer."

The documents found on the militants had been neatly laid out on a table in the mess. Amongst the documents were fake IDs of the militants and three diaries. I realised how futile it had been checking IDs of unknown people in my area. One of the diaries was full of poetry in Urdu. I had studied Urdu as a language in the National Defence Academy which came in handy now as I was able to read what was written in the diary. It was indeed all poetry written very very neatly in flawless Urdu calligraphy. Perhaps one of the militants was a romantic at heart. No wonder the romantic kinds are easy to subvert. Only a romantic at heart can romance ideas that call on people to embrace paths that lead to probable death.

The second diary too had a lot of poetry but also little bits of information including what appeared to be telephone numbers. A lot of the information was difficult to understand as it was coded. It showed places and people with names, coded to hide the actual identity of the person. However, the numbers were in the clear or so it appeared.

I decided that I should borrow the diary for a week and see what I could make of the information in it. As of then, everyone wanted to spend the afternoon celebrating and that is exactly how things proceeded.

Once the lunch was done, it was time for me to leave. But not before saying a hello to Ayaz over phone. It was a little unusual for Ayaz to not have contacted me. The firefight had happened and the word would have spread. I finally placed the call and his phone was again switched off. I really didn't know what to make of it. I couldn't have visited Ayaz's house in any case. I decided to wait and watch.

The same evening, however, I received a call from an unknown number. It turned out to be Ayaz.

"What happened to your phone? I was trying to call you since yesterday."

"I am sorry Saheb. I lost my phone sometime back. I have got a new one now. It is difficult to get a new number activated quickly.", said Ayaz.

"I know. I wanted to tell you that our operation in Kawari was a success. We got a few militants."

"Yes! I heard about it. Though, I thought you said Kawari was difficult to operate in."

"I don't know how it happened. But what a lot of people do not know is that someone got away. He had run towards village Batpura first. There is a chance that he got hurt. He was fired upon. I sense it could be Beg. Did you hear of anyone yesterday or today?"

"No Saheb!", replied Ayaz.

"Anyway, your prize is due. You can come by and collect it anytime."

"Ji shukriya! I will come by tomorrow."

The following morning I went to Handwara town for a routine liaison visit. Once in the town, I met senior police representatives and the magistrate. It was an additional task I had taken for the battalion since I was located closest to the town. By the time, I finished meeting all concerned and discussing any cases pertaining to the battalion, it was already 1 PM. As I stepped out of the police station onto the market place, I saw a familiar face. It was Riyaz who I was now meeting after nearly a year and a half. Riyaz was measured in his meeting with me as there were far too many people on the streets. He wanted to keep the meet and greet with me to the minimum under public eye.

"Why haven't you come to visit me all this time?, I asked.

"Saheb! I was sent to a different area and I have returned only recently.", replied Riyaz. "If it is okay, I will come and visit you this evening."

"Alright! I will wait for you!", I said sensing Riyaz's awkwardness in public. Meeting Army personal in public was always discomforting for a common Kashmiri.

I commenced my walk back to the op base with my team. Sometimes, walking is safer and it's definitely good for one's health. It took all of 30 minutes for my team to be back. The road itself was well sanitised and protected by the road opening party.

Riyaz indeed fetched up the same evening around 4 PM. I was happy to receive him.

"I am glad to see you. I was fearing you will disappear again.", I said.

"I am glad to see you too Saheb! Please don't embarrass me."

"You had helped me get Ayub. But you never met me ever since. There was a reward on his head that ideally you should have got."

"O! I thought that would have been claimed."

"No! Why do you say that? You never turned up.", I said to a very confused looking Riyaz.

"I am surprised too."

"What do you mean?"

"Actually the information on Ayub was given to me by someone else. He had told me that he would get in touch with you when the time comes and claim the reward."

"Who was that?"

"He is a resident of village Magam- Mohd Ayaz. Actually, he had provided me with the information and then wanted me to bring it to you."

"Oh! I am surprised too. Ayub was a high profile catch. Of course! At the time, I did not know Ayaz. How do you know him?", I asked.

"We both operated together for a while as mujahids before surrendering. We both hoped for a normal life looking for jobs doing even menial stuff. The civil society would not accept us. It was very difficult. The tanzeems ran their own agenda portraying us as villains. The civil society thought it is better to maintain a distance from us. We spent six horrible months looking for work. Those six months were terrible. Thankfully, for me, it was then that the government gave us a second chance by recruiting us as ikhwanis into the territorial Army. It created a dignified means of earning for me. Ayaz, however, was not so lucky. I got busy with my new found role in the society. Ayaz was then left all alone. I shudder to think how things would have been for Riyaz"

"Go on! Why did he give the information to you and not come to me directly?"

"One of course is because I had mentioned to him that you are on the lookout for Ayub and he said, he may know something about him. So, I believe when he learnt something he chose to tell me. Additionally, I believe you had recently then conducted a successful operation. Ayaz wanted to feed you the information. He trusted you to deliver successfully."

"How is it that Ayaz knows about all this? I can believe that you would know since you were based in Handwara and information flow is easy to come your way. Ayaz being in Magam cannot have similar access to information."

"Even I don't know how he gets all the information. He is perhaps still well connected with people from our active days. He had a knack for maintaining good relations."

"Could be! It takes quite an effort to do so. I wonder what kept him going?"

"A lot of it was in desperation I think. He was ostracised from the society. People have at a personal level been cordial with him but collectively they cannot engage with him. In public, definitely not. People cannot employ him. Perhaps in desperation, he would have reached out to his old friends. I have quietly helped him with money to see him through some difficult times. I wondered how he would survive long. But could never ask. Learning about his problems would have required me to do something about it and I wasn't sure if I could handle that."

"I understand! Anyways, now that you are back, do maintain contact and let me know what I can do for you."

"Ji Saheb! Jai Hind!"

With that Riyaz walked out and coincidentally at that very moment, Ayaz walked in. On the way, Ayaz and Riyaz stopped momentarily and exchanged pleasantries in Kashmiri clearly out of earshot range for me or anyone else in the base. Not that anyone understood Kashmiri in the first place.

"How are you, Ayaz?"

"Saheb! I am fine. How are you?"

"I am fine, but why do I see you walk awkwardly?"

"Saheb! I had slipped and fallen couple of days back. One of my knees is badly bruised and paining."

"Oh! How did it happen?"

"Nothing much Saheb! Some dogs got after me and started to chase me. I had to run and it was a little dark. I slipped and hurt my knee."

"I hope you are taking care of it."

"Ji Saheb!"

"Alright! I have only today learnt from Riyaz that the information on Ayub's whereabouts was in reality delivered by you. I am surprised to learn about your reach in these matters."

"Ji Saheb! It was a lucky break. I learnt about it from someone who was casually talking about him in the Magam market place with friends. He didn't know I was standing nearby and overheard their conversation. Only a few days earlier, Riyaz had told me about you. I thought it right to pass it on to you through Riyaz. I didn't believe you would believe me if I told you so in our first meeting ever."

"I understand that. Anyway, your information on Kawari was correct and we had a successful operation."

"That is good news Saheb! But news travels rather fast here in Kashmir. After all, there is not much else for the people to talk about. People are also happy about it. Those two who were visiting the village regularly had become quite a nuisance for the villagers."

I knew that was a standard response now. You get rid of some militants and the local villagers call it good riddance almost always but no one comes forth otherwise. Is it for the fear of the gun? Or is it just about sounding right?

"Haven't we heard that before on many occasions?"

"Yes! Perhaps people come to terms rather quickly. They want to see the silver lining always."

"How well do you know Riyaz?"

"Riyaz and I met at the training camp having gone across in 1995. Picking up the gun was so fashionable then.

We underwent training together and generally hit it off well being from the same general area. He was much better built and a lot fitter than me. He was strong while I was of a smaller composition and therefore agile.", recollected Ayaz. "We crossed back after the training with a gun feeling all powerful. We even operated together along with some of the other boys then. Of course, then things were easier. The Army had not built up in numbers like today and police was on the back foot. Most confrontations took place with unarmed civilian dissent. Then times changed and the Army presence increased. Life became difficult. Yielding the gun was not just glamorous but also fraught with risk. Families that were benefitting from our kinds became worried about our lives. Then the government offered us an olive branch and many of us took it. All along, somehow the two of us, have been together, barring a few times in between. In that sense, we have been thick. There were a few instances where we were caught inside a jungle surrounded by security forces when it appeared we may not survive. But together we helped each other get out. So, you can say we have trusted each other and looked out for each other."

"Well! That is quite something. Tell me where was Riyaz serving over the last one year or so?"

"Oh! He was here in Handwara. Sometimes, he was working on areas further south but he spent most of his time in Handwara itself."

That was strange because I remembered Riyaz telling me otherwise.

"Why would Riyaz lie to me? Or if he was telling the truth, why would Ayaz lie to me? Is Ayaz mistaken?", I thought to myself.

I figured confronting Riyaz on the matter may help me understand things better. I was intrigued.

"Coming to Kawari, on the night we struck, there were actually more than two militants. Luckily, we got them but someone who was leading them got away. I am still wondering if it could be Beg."

"I do not know how that happened. I only knew about the two who were coming in frequently. Perhaps, they were assigned to receive some others there. And as luck would have it, you struck on the very night. I will like to think it as a lucky strike."

"Yeah! Lucky but not without the pains involved in making it happen.", I corrected.

"Ji Saheb! But how did you do it?"

I only stared at Ayaz for a moment and then looked away pretending to have not heard Ayaz. Of course, Ayaz understood that he was not supposed to ask that question. I never told him even though I wanted to brag about every operation or at least the successful ones.

Ayaz left with his reward for the information provided. I knew my reward was being alive. I could not demand it but if considered worthy of it, the superior officers may cite me for a gallantry award. Gallantry awards were easier to come by if one got shot. In a world so competitive, a gun shot wound gave one an edge - those who martyred in the line of duty were of course in a different league - no one could morally ask them for evidence of bravery or sacrifice. In contrast, I was happy, that I and my men were in good shape and alive. Sometimes being alive is reward enough. But for me, it was important that some of my men who exhibited human values of a higher order were duly recognised. I decided to take up the matter with Haider accordingly.

As of now, I was a little puzzled with the day's interactions with Ayaz and Riyaz. I decided to call Riyaz over the next day again. This time I wanted to know his side of the story.

Riyaz came as planned. The pleasantries quickly exchanged, Riyaz and I settled down for a chat.

"How well do you know Ayaz?"

Riyaz was taken aback. He assumed I knew they were very close.

"Why do you ask Saheb?"

"Well! I want to know. Yesterday, after you left, he told me you were stationed at Handwara itself and did not go anywhere as you told me yesterday. So, one of you lied and I was wondering who and why?"

"Saheb! I indeed was sent on deputation to Langaite and also Sopore. I was indeed out of Handwara for nearly eight months. I did visit my village but those were short day trips and I did little more than meet my family and look into their needs."

"OK! So why would he tell me otherwise?", I asked.

"I have no idea Saheb! I even spoke to him over phone a couple of times from those places."

I was wondering why Ayaz would lie then.

"Could it be that Ayaz said so to distance me from Riyaz? Why would he do that?", I thought.

"So, how close have you been?", I asked.

"We have known each other for a long time since we met in the training camp across. We even crossed back together. We have been together in some risky operations. In one such operation, we were surrounded by security forces inside a jungle. Luckily, I and Ayaz got out of there alive. However, when we made a dash for our lives, somehow he got spotted and drew some fire while I had it relatively easy. He maintains to this day that he attracted the attention of the security forces on purpose to help me escape. Out of obligation forced on me by him ever since, I have to continue to repay the supposed favour to this day. There were more such situations thereafter, where I had to assume more risk than him. Somehow, I survived. But Ayaz makes me carry that obligation to this day as if it cannot be evened out and repaid."

"This sounds more like bullying to me. Ayaz's personality does not come across to be one of a bully. You did not think of confronting him?"

"I did but his language and tone then changed significantly. He even gets abusive and aggressive while trying to rub in my lack of gratitude towards him for saving my life. Personally, I have not been able to go to that level of rudeness. I have always chosen harmony over discord.", said Riyaz. "He has been particularly bitter since a year or so after the surrender. While most of us found employment with the security forces, he chose to work outside but the civil society has not been allowed to be kind towards those who surrender. People like Riyaz are an example for others in militant tanzeems as a caution against surrendering. It is actually working out well for a lot of youngsters today as they do not want to join militant tanzeems at all barring a few who get exposed to subversion very early in life. But yes! Ayaz has been bitter ever since. People like me who have been his old friends, therefore, carry a sense of pity and obligation towards him even though he is squarely responsible for his plight."

"How much is enough money to lead a fair life for someone like Ayaz?", I asked.

"For someone like Ayaz who already owns a house and doesn't really have a family, even Rs. 3000 a month is comfortable."

"He gets more than that for the work he does now."

"Yes sir! But only now. For quite sometime, no one believed him and before that no one afforded him any work."

"I see. He has reasons to be bitter and maybe that is why he could be possessive of me. Perhaps that is why he could say anything to distance you or anyone who may become a competition for him."

"People like us find it difficult to lead a normal life. Perhaps the only way it would become normal for us is when the militants and the militancy are no more. It is only then that we will become acceptable to the society."

"I understand. That is why you are doing your best to get rid of these militants."

"Yes Saheb! I think I will speak to Ayaz on why he had been lying about me."

With that the meeting ended. I now had time to myself. I had been exposed to new facets to Ayaz's personality. Ayaz was surely more complicated and smarter than he appeared. To me now, he had evolved from an unsuspecting simpleton who wanted power to someone who simply wanted rehabilitation to now someone who had figured the means of survival. The transformation had been swift and driven by the circumstances. Ayaz must have had a rough time coming back after the surrender. Expecting a normal life, all he would have received is ostracisation from the society. Even his friends and family would have been compelled to distance themselves from him in public. For Ayaz, it would have been a situation where all would have been lost overnight - family, friends and most importantly the gun and the power that came alongside. But that Ayaz had survived, spoke highly of his resilience.

I felt that I should visit Ayaz in his village even though it was against protocol of interacting with someone who worked as an information source for me. In the meantime, Riyaz was on his way to confront Ayaz before heading back to Handwara.

The following morning, I was in Magam. Accompanied by Shakeel- the local Company Commander, I and my team were pretending to conduct a routine familiarisation cum search operation in part of the village Magam - the side that included Ayaz's house. The idea of course was to meet Ayaz in his den. I really didn't know why I was doing it for I could have always called Ayaz over. But something told me I needed to disturb the waters that Ayaz lived in.

When my team finally reached Ayaz's house, I realised it was a below average house in the village built with meagre resources. One could not correctly guess when was the last time the house had been painted. It was a small house with just three rooms in all with the standard courtyard and a small barn and a shit box in one corner. On seeing me, Ayaz appeared a little tentative and not entirely comfortable. While my team members entered Ayaz's house to carry out a routine search, I and Ayaz stood outside in the courtyard chatting. There was no one else in his house. Ayaz was a loner and therefore, perhaps a risk taker.

"So, how was your meeting with Riyaz yesterday?", I asked.

"It went fine Saheb!", said Ayaz sensing I knew all about it.

"He tells me you lied about him."

"No Saheb! There must have been a misunderstanding.", replied Ayaz. "I was genuinely under the impression that he was in Handwara all along. Maybe because I met him once or twice in Handwara. I realise it was a mistake."

"Hmm! You had me worried otherwise! I was wondering why would you lie to me?"

"I would never lie Saheb. Never to you!"

"Anyways! I had come visiting Magam, so I thought I will pay you a visit. Calling you to the Magam camp would have been risky. I rather not spend more time here. There are other things Riyaz told me about you. We will discuss when you come visiting."

With that, I walked into Ayaz's house. The house interiors were a huge improvement over the exteriors. It was well furnished and comfortable. For putting up a show, I had to pretend we were actually there for a search. Hence, I looked around casually and then left.

I then proceeded to search another five houses in the village and returned to my op base. I wondered what was odd about Ayaz's house. Did I see something or was I imagining things?

On reaching the op base, I got busy with other administrative issues and put my mind to rest. It took me three more days to remember what had transpired in Magam and hence, decided to call Riyaz to figure how his meeting with Ayaz had gone. It was ten in the morning and Riyaz's phone was answered in the third attempt. But this time, it was not Riyaz on the other side but a female voice that answered.

"What do you want?"

"I wanted to speak with Riyaz."

"Riyaz is no more. Don't you know?", came the reply.

I was shocked beyond words. "How is that possible? Riyaz was always so careful.", I thought.

I called up the Company Commander at Handwara. Riyaz had been called by a friend to his village - Bakiakar the evening before last. Riyaz duly went to meet his friend. Once in the village, unarmed Riyaz was apprehended by a set of militants - who briefly tortured him and then shot him before scooting from the scene. The friend had been forced to make the call. Riyaz had been held responsible for the death of Ayub - the tanzeem had it finally figured.

I was aggrieved and felt compelled to visit Riyaz in his village. But I knew it instantly that, that would only make matters worse for his family. Beseeched with emotions, I shed a tear or two. But then the training had hardened me enough to be able to overcome my emotions. I wondered if Ayaz knew and began to frantically dial his number only to find the cell phone switched off.

"May be Ayaz is at Riyaz's funeral!", I guessed.

Ayaz remained unreachable for the entire day. I kept dialling Ayaz's number again and again so much so that I could now remember the number verbatim.

The sequence of Ayaz's number not being reachable continued the following day as well. When it continued into the third day, I decided to visit Ayaz in his village yet again - protocol be damned. On returning to Ayaz's house, I learnt that Ayaz too had gone missing. His house was somehow open and when I entered, it was nearly the same as I had seen it a few days earlier. It is also then that I realised, since those were now conspicuous through their absence, the missing pair of fur lined snow boots that had been lying in one corner of the house. It is then that I realised, what I had found odd about Ayaz's house.

Ayaz was gone, number of theories remained in my mind.

"Was his cover blown too like that of Riyaz?"

"Was someone observing frequent visits by both Ayaz and Riyaz to the op base?"

"Or was Ayaz hand in glove with the militants?"

I was intrigued and ordered my team to thoroughly search the house. This time the search was for real.

The search yielded some interesting literature - books of poetry, strong combinations of battery cells, coins that were foreign belonging to Afghanistan or Pakistan and a stack of dry batteries. I ordered for it all to be collected and carried back to base. A list was prepared and the house handed over to the village lambardar.

"Could it be that Ayaz was really upto something more than bearing the pitiable appearance?" I remembered what Riyaz had always warned me about, "Not everything was as it appeared to be!"

I immediately headed to the battalion headquarters to meet Aslam.

"I want to see all transmissions by Beg off late."

"Sir! Beg last made a transmission five days back. He claimed to have found at least one informer responsible for Ayub's death."

"Oh God! If only I had learnt of it earlier. We could have saved Riyaz."

"Then he did not make any transmission until two days back when he could be heard talking about reuniting with old friends after long. But this transmission was not the usual shouting in our ears kind. It was distant as if made from some 15-20 kilometres away with noise in the background. It appears Beg is on the move finally."

"OK thanks! Do let me know if you hear Beg on the radio again."

With that I returned to base.

I awaited anxiously for Beg to resurface but it was not to be. For seven straight days now, Beg had not been heard. He had apparently earned his passage back across the border or was now operating in a different part of the valley.

It was one fine morning that I once again spotted the diary obtained from the militants in the Kawari episode lying on my table. I opened it and began flipping through the pages to arrive on one that had a couple of numbers written in Urdu. I began to decipher the numbers into English recollecting my knowledge of Urdu from the academy days. The numbers were actually telephone numbers written vertically with one sequence that appeared rather familiar for it belonged to Ayaz. I was now convinced. That Ayaz was indeed hand in glove with the militants as well and could very much be doubling up as Beg. He could have orchestrated everything. He was the one who was 'managing the environment'.

I was now seething with anger. Ayaz had been playing a rather dangerous game of taking people's lives at will. I had luckily gotten away a few times myself and had lived to see this day. It could otherwise pretty much have been the other way around. Ayaz could have lived to game on while I would have long since gone.

All along where I felt I was in control, I was actually being played with, while lives were being lost and one person drew immense pleasure out of it all.

I immediately called for everything that had been confiscated from Ayaz's house. I began to slowly go over the books and literature found. As soon as I had picked up the first book, a note fell out of it written in Urdu, addressed to me. I was surprised for it was uncommon to find people who would write in Urdu.

"Dear Maqbool Saheb! I know you will eventually find this and read it. You are amongst the few who can in the Army. I could sense you were inching closer to my true identity and hence, I had to leave. Yes! I double up as Beg. I enjoyed working with you and even trying to get you. Your reliance on your military drills saved you every time and that is perhaps my only defeat. I know you follow rules but if you really want to get me, you will have to grow to think like me. The clues are all there in these books. It will take special talent to decipher those. Come and get me if you can. I know it is beyond you as of now but then you have already surprised me a few times."

I knew a couple of years down the line, the entire Army hierarchy would have changed in the area. Besides me, no one really knew Ayaz or even the contents of the note I had just read. For every new Commander, it is a fresh start. Ayaz could pretty much return and be upto his usual antics. I felt cheated and angry at the same time. I had considered Ayaz to be a close confidant. Speaking to him on an almost daily basis had created a strong liking for him. Part of my success, I owed to Ayaz. And Ayaz was actually only playing with me. Ayaz was responsible for many deaths and I felt compelled to avenge a few of those. I knew a little about Ayaz but it appeared that Ayaz knew a lot more about me.

Going after Ayaz required special approvals within the Indian Army and maybe even beyond going into other agencies that worked in managing affairs across the borders. It was no simple thing to do and achieve. And even before I could get necessary approvals, I had to first formulate a plan. A plan is what I did not have as of now. I didn't even know what Ayaz was upto.

I then looked at the literature lying in front of me and read the note again. I knew Ayaz had challenged me to do something I had no idea about. But if I wanted to do it, I would have to grow, learn to think beyond just the way a soldier does, maybe transform entirely. But first I had to figure out where Ayaz was headed. I somehow knew Ayaz would not lie to me. If he said the answers were all there in front of me, they must be.

The winters were fast arriving, the dogs were barking at night but this time it was the leopards who had ventured down from the mountains in search of food. The dogs were being hunted down.